secrets in september

Endorsements

The characters were funny, and I enjoyed reading about how they solved a huge mystery at the end. I just couldn't put this book down. I had to see what would happen next! It was a very entertaining and exciting book.
—**Emily S.**, age 11

Secrets in September was my favorite book that I read recently. It is a great book about Will, and his sister Wendy, who go on daily and hilarious adventures with their friends to solve the mystery of who was giving kids $50.00 bills. I would recommend this book to my friends in middle school. It had me at the edge of my seat wondering who was sending those notes! Looking forward to a second book.
—**Gabriel B.**, age 11, 6th Grader

It was a delightful treat to share this book with my son, as we tried to discover who the mysterious mastermind might be. As we read together, I was equally as engaged and drawn into the story. From the perspective of parent and Theology Teacher, I was pleased with the spiritual dimension of the story that taught my child about the sacraments, worship, and service. I highly recommend this book in helping young readers understand the true value of compassion and forgiveness.
—**Sonali Santiago-Borges,** Parent and High School Theology Teacher

secrets in september

DOREEN MCAVOY

PUBLISHING THE POSITIVE
Plymouth, Massachusetts

Copyright Notice

Cover and Interior Design: Derinda Babcock
Editor(s): Bobbie Temple, Deb Haggerty
Author Represented By: WordWise Media Services

PUBLISHED BY: Elk Lake Publishing, Inc., 35 Dogwood Drive, Plymouth, MA 02360, 2021

Library Cataloging Data

Names: McAvoy, Doreen (Doreen McAvoy)

Secrets in September / Doreen McAvoy

136 p. 23cm × 15cm (9in × 6 in.)

ISBN-13: 978-1-64949-280-7 (paperback) | 978-1-64949-281-4 (trade paperback) | 978-1-64949-282-1 (e-book)

Key Words: Middle-grade; mystery; school; church; family; friendship; ten commandments

Library of Congress Control Number: 2021940404 Fiction

Dedication

Dedicated with love and gratitude to my parents,
Eileen and Kevin Hartigan

Acknowledgments

I am grateful to God for giving me the opportunity to meet many wonderful people through this story.

I would like to thank Deb Haggerty and the ELPI team for their editing and support during the publishing process.

I am also lucky to work with Michelle Lazurek and WordWise Media Services. You have all been a blessing to me!

I would like to thank my beta readers, Emily and Gabriel, and their parents, for volunteering their time and offering to read the story through a Christian lens.

Thank you to my husband, Greg, and sons, Patrick, Greg, Chris, and Ryan for being my greatest fans—I love you!

Chapter 1

Will Abbott dropped his sleeping bag and pillow in his bedroom and trotted downstairs to the kitchen to join his mother and sister.

"Good morning." Mrs. Abbott smiled, waving him in. "Wendy was just telling me about last night."

"Yeah, how was Kimberly's party?" Will looked at his blonde twin.

"Fun. We played Truth or Dare. When it was Lili's turn, she chose truth." Wendy turned to her mother. "She told us her deepest wish was to get her ears double pierced for her thirteenth birthday."

Will recognized the hope in Wendy's tone—their own thirteenth birthday was only two weeks away.

Mrs. Abbott glanced at Wendy. "Well, if Lilianna wants to get her ears double pierced, maybe she should add that to her bedtime prayers. Will, did you have fun at Brandon's? How is Mrs. Lang feeling? The new baby is due soon."

"Okay, I guess. She watched a movie with us and went to bed. Then we just ... hung around." Will noticed Wendy glaring at him.

"Well, sounds nice. With all those sisters, I bet Brandon hopes for a brother this time." Mrs. Abbott grabbed her car keys. "I'm off to the grocery store. I hope you're almost done with your summer reading. School starts next week." She left without waiting for an answer.

Will settled in a chair across from his sister and tilted his head. "So ... what did you choose? Truth or Dare?"

"Truth—and good thing too. Samantha told me my dare would have been to ring the doorbell of the old Mayfield mansion."

Will scoffed. "That place has been empty for years. The Mayfields disappeared the night of the fire that destroyed the Jamison house. Some people even say Percy Mayfield started the fire over an old feud—although the rumor was never proven."

Wendy hugged herself and shuddered. "Still scary, though." She studied Will. "Are you sure you guys only hung around last night?"

"Yeah, why?" He tried to avoid Wendy's stare as he got up and walked across the kitchen to pour himself a glass of orange juice.

"There was a loud crash in Kimberly's yard last night outside the playroom window." Her green eyes scrutinized him. "It's funny how you always seem to have a sleepover at Brandon's whenever I'm at a party." She waited for an answer, hands on her hips.

Will grinned and stared at his feet.

"And funny how Brandon only lives three houses away from Kim—and likes her."

"How did you know?"

"Remember last year when he tried to give her a secret valentine, but she recognized his handwriting?"

"Oh yeah." Will chuckled.

"And funny how you, Brandon, and Jack always seem to know our secrets." Her big, green eyes demanded an answer.

Will was thankful when their dog, Buster, barked to announce he needed to pee.

"Gotta take care of Buster." Will scooted out the back door and escaped his sister's scrutiny—for the moment.

Chapter 2

Will knew he had heard his sister's voice float from Kimberly's window the night before.

"Truth ... I hope Derek Harrison will be in my class this year," followed by their giggling.

Derek Harrison ...

Will groaned aloud as he trudged toward Brandon's house with Buster trailing behind. "That's what I get for eavesdropping."

"Hey," Brandon said from his upstairs window, his mop of curly brown hair still wet from the shower. "I'll be right down."

Will toed the dirt as he waited. His foot hit something hard. He picked up a small stone. Squinting in the morning sun, he pulled a small magnifying glass from his pocket to search for unusual markings on his find. Seeing the stone was worthy of his rock collection, he pocketed the new piece for further examination as Brandon came out of his house. "You have to work today?" Will noted the stiff khakis Brandon only wore to church or when he had to work at his dad's car dealership—always with his beloved, dirty-white, hi-top sneakers.

"Yup." Brandon bent to pat Buster. "Listen ... about last night ... we have to be more careful. We almost got caught."

"Yeah, Wendy was grilling me. I think she knows we were listening—and they heard the crash when you fell off my shoulders."

"Let's just get pizza next time." Brandon grabbed his bike. "I gotta go. The dealership gets busy on Saturdays." Brandon punched Will's arm. "Dude, cheer up."

"Easy for you to say. You're not going to have Derek Harrison for a brother-in-law. Why can't Wendy just like you—or Jack?"

"Wouldn't be right. We're like brothers to her. Besides, Derek's an okay kid. You should be happy she doesn't like Beefy Boris." Brandon hopped on his bike and started to peddle.

"You should change your shoes."

"What? Never." Brandon zoomed off.

Will sighed. The last Saturday of summer vacation and Brandon and Jack were busy. *I guess I could hang out with Wendy—unless she is on the phone gabbing with someone. But maybe I shouldn't risk another interrogation.*

Will walked two and a half blocks home with Buster leading the way, and he thought about Derek Harrison and why the kid bothered him so much other than he was better in most everything than Will.

"He beats me at everything," Will said to his shaggy mutt who seemed more interested in getting home to a big bowl of water and his shady spot in the yard.

Almost home, Will slowed as he passed an abandoned lot—the site of a house fire which had claimed the lives of three members of the Jamison family. A tangle of trees, bushes, and tall weeds screened the property from the street. Will and his friends often wondered what lie beyond the overgrowth but resisted the urge to explore. Now, pulling Buster along, he left the sidewalk to peer in but jumped back when branches parted, and someone stepped out.

"Oh, Will, you startled me."

He exhaled when he recognized his elderly neighbor, Mrs. Larson. Buster's tail whipped back and forth as her miniature dachshund scooted out from behind her.

Mrs. Larson tugged at her pant leg caught on a briar. "What on earth were you doing?"

"Uh … just … nothing really …"

"You're probably wondering what I was doing in there."

"No, I ..."

She glanced over at the dogs frolicking. "Petunia and I still come to leave flowers."

Will cleared his throat. "Um ... what's back there? I mean ... I know about the fire ..."

"Oh, there's nothing left—just rubble." She shook her head. "So tragic ... the fire devastated our town. Did you know I was the one who called the fire department?"

Will shook his head, open-mouthed.

"Yes—twelve years ago. The day was a beautiful ... a Sunday afternoon. I heard someone banging on my front door. I looked out my window and saw Percy."

"Percy Mayfield?" Will furrowed his brow.

"Yes. He was yelling about a fire at the Jamison's house and for someone to call for help. The fire trucks arrived quickly but too late. They said the family was overcome by smoke before they could escape." She dabbed the corner of her eye with her sleeve. "Walter Jamison was a friend of mine."

"I'm sorry."

"And of course, I knew his son and daughter-in-law as well." She sighed and managed a smile. "It's a miracle their baby survived. Authorities found her outside. She's about your age now."

"Where is she?"

"She lives in California with her uncle. Come, Petunia!" She tugged the leash. "I'd better be getting back, Will. Your mother is picking me up for the block party committee meeting soon."

Will watched her go. *I should have asked Mrs. Larson about the Jamison's feud with the Mayfield family,* he thought. He had asked his mother about the story once, but she seemed reluctant to discuss neighborhood gossip.

As he jogged up his driveway, Will noticed something green on the black mulch. He stooped and picked up a twenty-dollar bill. What luck! Smoothing the cash out over his knee, he looked around. Strange how he found the bill out in the open. He half expected someone to jump out from behind the bushes and laugh at him for falling for a joke, but no one did. Not knowing what else to do, he put the cash in his pocket next to his new stone.

He unlatched the back gate for Buster, turned the corner to the garage, and stopped. Brandon's bike lay in front of him. He looked up and saw his friend at the door talking to Wendy. He couldn't hear what Brandon was saying, but he saw the serious expression on Wendy's face. Will rushed over to them. Brandon grabbed his arm.

"Come on, get your bike," he said. "Someone trashed the car dealership last night!"

Chapter 3

Will sped off with Brandon toward the dealership.

"I'm coming too!" Wendy jumped on her bike and caught them at a red light.

"... and they broke into the office and stole the cash box from the desk." Brandon tried to catch his breath.

When the light turned green, they rolled into the dealership lot where a small crowd of onlookers had gathered. Wendy saw her friends from school and joined them.

"Wow." From behind the police tape, Will gaped at the crowd, the squad cars, and the smashed showroom window. Will and Brandon dropped their bikes and walked over to where Mr. Lang was finishing his report with Officer Travers.

"Don't worry, Bill, we'll find that money," the earnest officer said. "We received several calls last night ... kids being derelict. Someone sprayed creepy graffiti on the old train trestle and stole a few bikes—plus a report of someone snooping around the old Mayfield mansion." He turned to Will and Brandon. "Wasn't you guys, I hope?" Wide-eyed, they shook their heads.

"Nah, just kidding ..." he said. "How are you doing anyway? Eighth grade this year, right? Fun stuff ..." Officer Travers laughed as Brandon groaned and followed his dad inside.

The money. Will clutched his twenty-dollar bill. Had the bill come from the stolen cash box? He watched Officer

Knobbel, Knobby as he was known around town, scratch his bald head and scan the crowd.

As the crowd broke, Will's gaze fell upon a lone figure standing at the edge of the parking lot, hands casually in his front pockets. Derek Harrison.

Derek stared back. For one awkward moment, Will debated acknowledging or ignoring him. Then Derek pulled a hand from his pocket and gave Will a brief salute as he turned and walked away with the rest of the crowd. Will observed him, his own hand feeling heavy.

Wendy pulled up next to him. "Was Derek Harrison waving to you?"

Will shrugged.

"He is nice, you know," Wendy said as they started riding home.

"Yeah." Eager to change the subject, he told her about the report of trespassing on the Mayfield property. "Good thing you didn't have to complete your dare last night."

"Maybe someone else was playing Truth or Dare."

"Or," Will said, "maybe the visitor was one of the Mayfields." He told her about his conversation with Mrs. Larson.

"Percy Mayfield alerted the neighbors? It's rumored he started the fire. Why would he start a fire and then run for help?"

"I was wondering the same thing." They stopped at an intersection. "Come on, let's ride past." Will twisted his handlebars, ready to take the detour.

"Past the Mayfield's house?" Wendy's eyebrows shot up. "You just said one of them might be hanging around."

"I was only kidding, and we'll be safe during the day." His mind made up, he pedaled off.

With a sigh, Wendy followed. They rode along the outskirts of the neighborhood where the homes became fewer and the road bumpier and more difficult to navigate.

"I don't like this," Wendy said. "I feel like we're alone out here."

"Once we pass the house, the road loops back to—look, the police!"

They slowed as the turrets of the mansion became visible over the treetops. They rolled by the massive house, which was set back down a long driveway, and tried not to stare. In a patrol car parked in front, an officer noted them with a slight nod of his head. Once past, they followed the road back to their neighborhood.

"That is a sad house."

Will agreed. Strange, he thought, why would the police be parked outside?

Chapter 4

Over dinner, Will and Wendy recounted the day's events for their parents but omitted their excursion past the Mayfield mansion.

"Well, that's unfortunate. I'm surprised Bill hasn't called me about the robbery," said Mr. Abbott. "I was at the office all day. He'll definitely have to put in an insurance claim." He reached for the last piece of barbecued chicken.

"I'm sure he'll call you, honey," Mrs. Abbott said. "They do have a new baby coming and all."

He nodded as he munched on a chicken leg. "Any idea how much money was taken?"

Wendy shook her head as she helped her mom clear the table. "I only heard the cash box was stolen."

Will shrugged and said nothing.

"Well, did he say—" Mr. Abbott's cell phone vibrated. "Hello? … Yes, Bill, I'm glad you called. Sorry to hear about the trouble …" He left the room.

Will sat alone at the table with Buster who waited for a morsel. Will tossed him the last bit of chicken as he wondered again if the twenty-dollar bill he found was stolen from the cash box. He patted his front pocket where the money was safely tucked away and felt the lump of the stone he found. He pulled the small rock out, along with his magnifying glass. The stone seemed average-looking until the late day sun illuminated a pattern on the face. When he held the stone steady at just the right angle, Will could see an L shaped pattern of crystals. Cool, he thought, L for lucky. He stuck the stone back in his pocket and thought about what to do with the rest of the afternoon.

"I'm going out for a ride, Mom."

"Be back before dark."

"Want to come, Wen?"

Wendy looked outside with longing but shook her head. "I want to finish summer reading."

Will nodded, having finished his already. He hopped on his bike and headed toward the park hoping to find some kids shooting baskets. He rode out of his way, down Maple Street where Ava Flores lived. *She is one of the nicest girls in my class.* But he sped past her house not knowing what he would say if he did see her.

Will stopped at the nearby intersection. He noticed a large roundish object moving across the road. He inched closer and saw the lump was a turtle. He tapped it with his sneaker in case the thing snapped at him.

"That's a box turtle."

Will heard a soft voice behind him and turned to see Ava.

"They don't bite. I have one. He's probably looking for the pond."

"Uh … yeah," Will said, trying not to sound dumb. "I can take him. I'm headed over to the park now anyway."

"Okay, watch him. I'll go get a box." She ran the short distance to her house and was back before any cars came. Will kept watch for any approaching traffic while Ava gently nudged the turtle into the box with the toe of her sneaker.

"There," she said, giving the box to Will. "Are you sure you can hold him?"

"Yup, no problem," Will said, confident about his bike riding ability.

"Okay, well, I guess I'll see you at school," Ava said with a wave.

"Yeah, maybe we'll be in the same class." The words tumbled out before he could shut his mouth. Stupid, stupid, stupid. He grimaced as he rode away.

He entered the park as dusk settled in and hurried down the path to the pond. He was eager to deliver the turtle and get home before he got in trouble, but he spotted someone near a grove of trees. Beefy Boris Bobrick!

He tried to sneak past unnoticed.

"Hey, Abbott! Wanna see something?" Boris called.

Boris chucked a rock at a tree. Will slowed as he heard a frightened chittering sound from a squirrel who jumped from the tree to a higher branch and scampered off to safety. Boris howled with laughter. Will shook his head in disgust. He continued down the path as he heard Boris yell, "Hey, watcha got in the box?" Will dumped the turtle into the pond before Boris approached. He ran back up the path and hopped on his bike.

Boris kept throwing rocks at the trees. "Hey, Abbott, maybe I'll see you in my class this year! Hey, say 'hey' to your sister!"

Chapter 5

"Come on, guys, time to get up! Don't make us late for church." The twins passed each other in the hall outside the bathroom.

"At least we still have another week before Sunday School starts." Will yawned and Wendy managed a sleepy nod.

A half hour later after dodging raindrops, they arrived at St. Therese's and sat in a pew directly behind the Lang family right on time for the opening hymn. Brandon turned and nodded at Will.

Will tried to focus, but Mr. Lang's presence in front of him proved distracting, especially with the twenty-dollar bill in his pocket. He considered several different scenarios where he could mention the subject of the missing money to Mr. Lang, but they all seemed lame. The fact remained he could have part of the dealership's stolen loot in his pocket.

Will forced his attention back to the service and tried to let the lector's soothing voice wash away his anxiety. The Bobrick family—minus Boris—sat in a pew across the aisle. The two younger Bobricks colored in, he suspected, the church hymnal—Mr. and Mrs. Bobrick oblivious to the matter. Will figured Boris still slept after an exhausting evening of terrorizing squirrels at the park. He did not want to think bad things about Boris, especially in church. So, instead, he tried to think good things about him. He thought all the way back to first grade. Nothing. Beefy Boris had always bullied others. Even back then, no animal, insect, or kid survived his meaty fists.

A sharp poke from behind startled Will from his thoughts. Jack Russell grinned at him as his family tiptoed into the pew.

"Terrier." Will smiled, whispering Jack's nickname. They exchanged a quick fist bump as he passed.

Will settled back and listened to the guest speaker, a missionary who spoke about his village back home in East Africa and the great faith of his people despite their desperate need for wells to provide clean water. Will glanced at his sister and saw her big green eyes filled with sympathy. When the ushers passed the collection basket around, she glared at their father until he threw in an extra ten-dollar bill. Will considered smuggling the twenty bucks out of his pocket and into the basket, but somehow, using the plight of the poor villagers to his advantage didn't seem right, not to mention immoral to give away money he might not own. Will sighed and decided to talk to Jack.

Chapter 6

On Monday morning, the sky dawned a fiery red, promising both clouds and sun, fitting for an event that signaled the end of joyous summer frolicking—the Labor Day block party.

Will came downstairs for breakfast and found his mother in the kitchen preparing a huge batch of her famous barbecue sauce for the baby back ribs their family contributed to the potluck feast.

"Eat cereal, please." Mrs. Abbott squeezed a bottle of ketchup into a large mixing bowl containing a heaping mound of brown sugar and her special combination of pepper flakes.

"Sure." Will reached over the mess on the counter for the cereal box and moved out of her way.

"… and good morning." She smiled. "The weather should clear up nicely for the block party later. Your dad, Mr. Lang, and some other helpers are setting up tables at Memorial Field right now. I'm sure they could use some extra muscle." She handed Will a spoon. "Are you ready for tomorrow? School supplies? Summer reading?"

"Yeah, I guess—and thanks for the sneakers. They're really cool." Will still couldn't believe his mom bought him the sneakers he had admired all summer but had feared asking her to buy because of the price.

"You're welcome, honey. I bought them on sale, plus I had a coupon. I know they're a little big, but your feet will grow—" She stopped stirring and looked at Will. He stared into his bowl, lost in thought.

"Mom, what would you do if you found money? Like … I don't know … a dollar?"

"One dollar?" She paused for a moment to look at him. "Well, I find dollars in the laundry all the time. I leave them on the laundry room shelf and they magically disappear."

"Okay." Will tried not to smile. "What if you found more than one dollar. What would you do then?"

"Honestly, I would try to find the owner. If I couldn't, I'd tell an authority … like the principal if I found some cash at school—or the police, maybe. Sometimes, they hold the money for a while. If no one comes forward to make a claim, they let you keep the cash. And if I could keep the money, I would donate some to the poor." She stirred her sauce.

Will paused. He shoveled the last mouthful of cereal in, pushed his chair back, and jumped up. "Okay, thanks. I'm going down to help with the setup." He ran out of the kitchen as his mother stared at him with a furrowed brow.

Walking to the block party setup gave Will more time to think about what to say to Mr. Lang. He bit his lip. If he had told the police about the cash he found, they could have investigated the clue.

Will approached the busy site. The helpers set up grills, arranged tables and chairs, and bustled under the keen supervision of Mrs. Larson and Petunia. Will's father held a phone to his ear with one hand—most likely speaking to a client, Will thought—and opened folding chairs with the other. Will searched for Mr. Lang's tall form but didn't see him at first. Then he spied him bent over a grill with a screwdriver in hand. Will considered turning around. Thoughts of his seventh-grade Sunday School teacher, Miss Chapman, popped into his head. Although he hadn't paid as much attention in class as he should have, he remembered her saying at least a hundred times to pray to the Holy Spirit for the courage to do the right thing.

"Okay fine, Miss Chapman," Will said to himself and then prayed as he strode up to Mr. Lang.

"Great timing, Will," Mr. Lang said. "Hold this for me a minute." He handed the screwdriver to Will and tried to straighten the grill lid from underneath.

"I found a twenty-dollar bill." Will blurted the words out. He closed his eyes and tensed, waiting for a verbal onslaught.

"Wow, lucky you." Mr. Lang reached for the screwdriver again without even looking up.

Will opened his eyes. "No, I mean ... I may have found stolen money from your ... your office."

Mr. Lang stood and looked at Will. "Why do you think so?"

"Well, I found the bill lying near my house right after the robbery."

"Hmm ... sounds like a coincidence. I'm sure your money did not come from the cash box. There were only fifty-dollar bills inside. See, usually people buy cars with credit, but sometimes they pay cash. Luckily, I had already deposited our weekly cash at the bank Friday afternoon, but a customer arrived before closing and put a cash deposit down on a used car. The robber stole the deposit."

"So-o-o ..."

"So, you are twenty dollars richer." Mr. Lang chuckled and patted Will on the back.

After helping set up the last of the chairs, Will still found himself smiling as he walked back home. Officer Knobby placed a police barricade at the street corner to redirect traffic away from the block party.

One more thing to do, Will thought.

"Yo, what's up, Will," the officer called.

"Um ... I just wanted to ask ... I found a twenty-dollar bill the other day. Do you know if anyone lost one?"

"Nope, we hardly ever get those kind of reports. If we did, I'd remember."

"Really?"

"Yup. If people lose a small amount of money, they usually blame themselves for their carelessness. Me?" He pointed to himself. "If I lose a ten or a twenty, I kick myself. Then I hope someone who needs cash finds what I left behind." He slammed the trunk of his police car. "Now, if you find a bike laying around, I'd like to know. You heard someone stole a few last Friday, right?"

Will nodded.

"Hey, your mom is bringing her ribs to the party later?" When Will nodded again, Knobby winked. "I might have to stop by then."

Knobby drove off and Will watched while patting the pocket where his twenty-dollar bill sat.

Chapter 7

"I'm walking with Kim." Wendy grabbed her purse, ready to head out the front door. The sound of the block party music drifted up the street. "Bye!"

"Wait, grab a bag from the counter. I can't take everything myself." Their mother rushed out of the kitchen with two bags of party snacks. "Here, these are light." She handed them to Wendy as Will came downstairs. "Will, can you bring the bags with the paper plates and tablecloths? I'll load the wagon with the food trays. Unfortunately, your dad will arrive a little late."

"Mom, isn't Labor Day supposed to celebrate people who work by giving them a day off?" Wendy adjusted the bags in her arms.

"Well, yes. I mean … usually. Not everyone can take the day off."

"Yeah," Will said. "Brandon will be late too because Lang's Auto Mall stayed open. I'm walking down with Jack."

"Don't worry—your dad won't take long. Listen, you two, stay safe. I'm concerned about some things happening around here. Know your surroundings, okay?"

"Got it," Will said. Wendy nodded.

"Weird," Wendy glanced back as they walked down the driveway. "Mom looked worried."

Will nodded. "Look, I see Kim." He pointed to Kimberly and Samantha Lee walking in their direction. Wendy ran to join them.

The sight of the police car in front of the Mayfield mansion had stuck with Will. He shook his head to clear the troublesome thought and headed to Jack's house.

Jack was already waiting outside. "Come on!" Jack said, tapping his foot.

Will grinned, knowing Jack's habits—never late to a party. Jack Russell, aka Terrier, fit his nickname perfectly due to his small stature, quick moves, smart wits, and abundance of energy.

As they walked to Memorial field, Will filled Jack in on the events of the last few days.

"It's weird the police were still at the Mayfield's the next day." Jack furrowed his brow.

"I thought so too."

"So, Mr. Lang lost out on money and has to have a bunch of glass replaced because of some punks?" Jack balled his fists.

"Yeah, well, he has insurance."

"Where's the graffiti? I want to take a look."

"I think you'd have to hike to the old train trestle in the woods," Will said, and then he told him about finding the money and the stone.

"Lemme see." Jack held out his hand. Will pulled out the twenty. "No, the rock. Dude, I know what a twenty-dollar bill looks like."

Jack held the stone up and squinted. "I don't see any crystals." He tossed the stone back. "Seems cool, though."

"Too cloudy." Will stuck the stone back in his pocket while they ran to the party where Jack's older brother, Jon, and Tommy Lee organized teams for a soccer game. Brandon finally arrived, and Will propelled him onto Kimberly's team with a good-natured shove.

The sun finally broke through when the soccer score was tied. The moms called everyone to dinner to feast on burgers, hot dogs, ribs, chicken, casseroles, and plenty of salads. Mrs. Larson entertained everyone with stories about the history of the neighborhood.

"The train would roll right through here." She pointed toward the woods. "The houses would shake and shudder something terrible." She shook her head. "I lost a few good pieces of china, for sure. But the train brought people, and the people needed houses, and here we are today."

"When did the train line shut down?" someone asked.

"Oh, twenty-five years ago. The event was big news." Mrs. Larson waved her hand. "The line had become useless. The old station needed repairs and we knew the trestle over the stream could collapse. So, they built a shiny new transportation center in Maple Grove to run the line through. Though only one town away, some people never understood the decision." Tears welled up in her eyes.

"My daddy tells the story the same way, Mrs. Larson." They turned to see Officer Knobby had arrived. He grinned. "Any leftovers?"

Everyone laughed.

"Come on," Jack said to Brandon and Will, his voice low. "I want to see the creepy graffiti on the train trestle."

Chapter 8

The three boys left the block party and ran to the edge of the grassy area and snuck behind some trees. Then they crept into the woods.

"Seems darker than usual in here," Will said as they walked down the path.

"The leaves are blocking the sunlight." Brandon held a branch up for Will to duck under.

Jack forged ahead, clearing away bushy ferns to keep the path passable. The farther they trekked, the darker and more overgrown the path became. Will tried to keep track of their direction but navigating became difficult. He wished he had his compass with him.

"Okay, which way?" Jack stopped. The boys saw how the dim path broke off into two equally dark and rough looking trails.

Brandon hesitated. "Maybe we should—"

Pop! Crack!

The boys froze upon hearing a twig snap. Someone was approaching from behind. Jack put his finger to his lips, bent over, and picked up a large branch. The boys crouched. They listened as whispers grew louder. Will was sure his friends could hear his heart pounding. He tensed his shoulders and held his breath.

"Ew-w-w, Kim, I just stepped on something squishy." Will heard his sister's voice and relaxed. Jack half-chuckled and lowered his branch while Brandon motioned to stay down and grinned, placing his finger to his lips.

Through the dim light, the figures of Wendy, Kimberly, and Samantha Lee approached.

"This is the only way they could have—"

The boys leaped out of the bushes and into their path. The three girls jumped back and screamed as the boys whooped with laughter.

"You guys are totally mean!" Samantha yelled, sending them into fresh hysterics.

"Well, why are you following us?" Brandon chuckled, wiping away tears.

Crashing through the brush, Jon and Tommy rushed into view. "We heard a scream." Tommy looked at his sister.

"They jumped out and scared us," Samantha said.

"They were following us," Jack shot back.

"None of you should be here right now anyway. Jack, Mom sent us to look for you guys," Jon said. "Fun's over. Let's go."

"No way! We want to see the graffiti on the train trestle."

"First of all, you're going the wrong way. The train trestle is that way," Jon said, pointing. "Second of all, the path is too dark now. Did any of you even bring a flashlight?" He pulled a small flashlight out of his pocket and shined the light around the forest. "See, you can't—"

"Wait!" Will said. He peered into the bushes. "Shine the light over by those trees again."

Jon pointed the flashlight.

"I see something behind the bushes."

The group walked over and Jack used his branch to push back the bushes. They stared at a pile of bicycles.

"Hey, Joey Alomar's bike," Tommy said, "—the orange one. Someone stole his bike the other night. Wow! How many bikes are in this pile?"

Wendy wrung her hands. "I think we'd better go tell someone." Everyone nodded and they jogged back along the trail in the faint light.

As they broke out of the forest and onto the grassy area, Will saw his mother's worried face and Mr. Lang talking to Knobby who held his police radio. The whole block party stalled upon seeing the missing kids, then breathed a collective sigh of relief.

The kids rushed over to their parents whose concern was replaced with reproach. Even Knobby frowned at them. "Why did you kids—"

"We found the stolen bikes," Will blurted, pointing, "in the woods!" His friends nodded.

Knobby clicked on his radio and called dispatch for a patrol car.

"We'll show you." Will turned back toward the woods.

"Oh, no you won't. We'll take over. You guys worried your folks sick."

Will glanced at his parents. "Sorry."

"We didn't mean to be gone so long," Wendy said.

"You actually weren't gone long," their father said. "We just didn't know where you were."

Knobby stepped forward. "We need to go in the woods, but we'll wait a bit for you folks to finish up here."

"Good," Mrs. Russell said, pointing to a wheelbarrow, "because I didn't fill all those water balloons for nothing."

Everyone cheered and grabbed a partner as the highlight of the afternoon, the annual water balloon contest, began. They all enjoyed dessert, soaking wet, and wrapped up the summer festivities as the police brought in lights to investigate the find in the woods.

Will pulled the wagon of leftovers as the Abbotts walked home together after helping to clean up.

"Mom, who would steal bicycles and dump them in the woods?" Wendy asked.

"I don't know, but I hope the theft was nothing more than a prank, and I repeat what I said earlier—please, be careful."

Will nodded, biting his lip as he trudged along behind, thinking about the first day of school.

Please, God, let all my friends be in my class, he prayed.

Chapter 9

Tuesday morning, Will stood with Brandon, Jack, and the rest of the student body in the Fern Valley Middle School gymnasium. The air buzzed with nervous energy as Principal Thomas read the class rosters for the new school year. One by one, classes filed out until only the eighth graders were left. Will looked around at the group and surprised, noticed how much everyone had changed over one summer. He leaned toward Jack and Brandon. "Micky O'Brien grew a foot."

Jack glanced over. "Yeah, but I'll still be able to guard him," he scoffed, already planning his lunchtime basketball game strategy.

Will saw Ava chatting with the girls from the soccer team, and Derek Harrison toward the back with another bunch of boys. He chuckled at Wendy and her friends, arms linked, as if daring anyone to separate them. He also noticed Boris, already sifting through an unattended backpack, no doubt trying to nab a snack.

Brandon nudged him. "Where are the eighth-grade teachers?"

Will followed his gaze to the front of the gym where the teachers had been gathered. Now, only one man stood with the principal.

"May I have your attention, please?" Principal Thomas's deep voice called everyone's attention forward.

"Welcome back. As I look at you, the new eighth-grade class, I can't help but think back to three years ago when you entered Fern Valley Middle School as fifth graders. You have grown and matured ...”

“I bet he says the same thing every year,” Brandon murmured as Jack crossed his arms and tapped his foot.

“We have had some changes over this summer,” Principal Thomas continued. “One of our eighth-grade teachers, Mrs. Harper, has retired.”

Will heard a quiet, “Yes!” from somewhere behind him and tried to look as innocent as possible when the principal frowned in his direction.

“And our other eighth-grade teacher, Miss Pierre, has been moved to fifth grade.” He paused for the expected groans. “In addition, and I expect this change will affect you most—your class size has dropped. So I see no need for two eighth-grade classes.” He paused to let the information sink in and smiled as realization dawned on their faces. “We will have one eighth-grade class this year, and I’d like to introduce your teacher, Mr. Lockwood.”

Everyone gasped—followed by cheers, squeals of joy, hugging, and fist bumps. The tension in the room broke while Principal Thomas finished with a sober reminder of school rules and responsibilities.

The eager students followed Mr. Lockwood out of the gym.

“I never had a guy teacher before,” Micky O’Brien whispered as they headed down the hall.

Will nodded. “Me either.”

Boris overheard and snickered. “Yeah, did you see his eyes? One blue, one brown? This is way cooler than having Mrs. Harper.”

“Boris!” Principal Thomas boomed from the rear. “Quiet in the hall, please.”

Mr. Lockwood led them into their classroom. “I will seat you in alphabetical order by last name.”

Will stepped forward but stopped when he heard, “Wendy Abbott.”

“Ha.” Jack nudged him. “Never had Wendy in your class.”

“Will Abbott.”

Will walked slowly to his seat behind Wendy's.

"Boris Bobrick."

"Here!" Boris pushed his way through to his seat behind Will's.

Will regretted that every year since first grade when Boris wasn't in his class, Boris had been in Wendy's class— and had sat directly behind her. He silently pledged to use his seat as a protective shield for his sister this year.

Mr. Lockwood called each student and gave them time to organize their desks and settle in. Will gazed around the classroom and noticed the walls and bulletin boards were bare. Mrs. Harper would have decorated, he thought. Will peeked back over his left shoulder to see Ava. She glanced up at the same time and smiled. He waved and turned around knowing his face would flush. He busied himself and then noticed Derek Harrison looking over in his direction. He was about to nod when he realized Derek wasn't looking at him. His gaze was on Wendy.

Oh, great, Will thought.

"Hey, Abbott, got a pencil?" Boris poked Will hard in the back.

Will sighed and handed one of his newly sharpened pencils over his shoulder.

Wendy glanced back at him. "We'll have a fun year."

"Yeah," Will mumbled, "great fun."

Chapter 10

"I'm happy you're both in the same class this year," Mrs. Abbott said at dinner.

"Yeah, we were all shocked," Wendy said, "and our new teacher is pretty nice."

"What's his name again?"

"Mr. Lockwood," Will said, scooping a little more baked ziti onto his plate.

"Where did he come from? How old is he?"

"He didn't tell us too much about himself. I think he had his hands full with Boris." Will sighed. "And that reminds me, I'll need some more pencils for tomorrow."

"Well, I guess I'll learn more at Meet the Teacher Night." The doorbell rang. Mrs. Abbott looked at her watch and jumped up. "Speaking of Boris," she said while clearing the dishes from the table, "Mrs. Bobrick is at the door right now."

"Mrs. Bobrick? Here?" Will dropped his fork. "Why?" Will ran for the stairs with Wendy close behind.

"Oh, no, you don't! Finish cleaning up in here, please. We'll be in the living room planning the Sunday School Welcome Back Picnic." She grabbed a stack of papers and rushed out as the doorbell rang again.

The twins raced to load their plates into the dishwasher. Then Wendy bolted upstairs. Will stopped to pat Buster whose sad eyes showed disappointment in the lack of leftover scraps.

"Next time, buddy." Will charged after Wendy but froze when he heard his mother's panicked voice loud and clear.

"Helene, hi! *Oh*, you brought the kids. Umm … no … no, the playroom is this way …"

The two youngest Bobricks burst into the kitchen followed by Mrs. Bobrick, her hair askew. She grabbed them by their shirt collars and hustled them out as Boris sauntered in.

"Hey, Abbott, what's up? Just finished dinner?"

Will noticed Boris eyeing the leftover ziti in a dish on the stove. "Uh … yeah, you hungry?"

"No, I ate," he said as he moved closer to the dish. "Where's your sister?"

"She's upstairs … busy … doing stuff."

"Oh, too bad. I wanted to show her this." Boris struggled to slide his oversized fist into his back pocket to pull out a crumpled bill. He flattened the money out on the kitchen table. Will tried to hide his surprise when he saw the fifty.

"Ever see one of these?"

Will stood silent. He didn't want to admit he hadn't.

"Where'd you get a fifty-dollar bill?"

Boris leaned forward. "At the park."

Will shrugged. "I found a twenty last week near my driveway."

Boris scoffed. "A twenty? Hah! A fifty is way better." He looked around the kitchen again. "And I might get more Friday night."

"How?" Will's eyes narrowed.

Boris sat back, but his gaze continued to dart around the room. He reached out to pet Buster but withdrew his hand when Buster growled.

Will jumped up. "I'd better bring him outside." He hustled Buster out the back door. Will wondered to himself. *Did Boris really find the fifty at the park? Was his money part of the loot stolen from Lang's Auto Mall?*

Will went back into the house. The kitchen was empty. Panic seized him and he bounded up the stairs. He pressed his ear to Wendy's bedroom door. He could hear her singing.

He ran back downstairs and peeked into the living room. The two younger Bobricks watched cartoons while his mother and Mrs. Bobrick hunched over their lists.

His mom paused. "Hi, honey."

"Uh, I was looking for Boris."

"Oh, he had to go." Mrs. Bobrick looked away. "He said to tell you goodbye."

Will nodded, feeling pretty sure Boris said nothing of the sort. "Okay, good night." He trotted upstairs to his own room and laid in bed. He was sure of one thing—Boris was up to no good.

Chapter 11

Will arrived at school late the next morning. With his head down, he handed Mr. Lockwood a late pass and slipped into his seat.

Wendy whispered to him. "I thought you were ready to go when I left. Did you forget your lunch?"

Will mumbled as he opened his math book, "Something like that."

Most of the morning had passed before Will realized the silence behind him. Hardly daring to hope, he cast a furtive glance over his shoulder. Boris's desk was empty. Will nodded at Lucas Coleman who sat two desks back.

"No Beefy," Will mouthed to Brandon, who grinned. As Will swung back around, he risked a glance at Ava and saw her watching him. She held up a small slip of paper and he smiled when he saw her goofy drawing of a turtle along with the words Save the Turtles underneath. She flipped the note around and he read the message on the back. Play soccer at recess. Will nodded, cheeks burning, and he faced front.

When the lunch bell finally rang, Will grabbed Jack and Brandon and directed them to a remote table in the far corner of the cafeteria.

"What?" Jack pressed. "Why were you late?"

Will shook his head. "I was looking for something." He glanced around and whispered. "You'll never guess who was at my house last night."

"Boris!" Brandon laughed at Will's deflated expression. "Wendy told Kim and Kim told me."

"Of course." Will sighed.

Jack frowned. "Wait … Boris? Why?"

Will leaned in. "This is crazy. He wanted to show off the fifty—"

Brandon held his hand up as three fifth grade boys approached their table.

"Arghhh! What?" Jack glared at them.

Unfazed, the smallest one stared at him. "Thanks for finding my bike."

Jack sat back. "Your bike?"

"Yeah, someone stole my bike last week. My mom was going to make me pay for a new one. But then you guys found the pile of bikes in the woods. Knobby told us." His friends bobbed their heads in agreement.

"Oh."

Will and Brandon stared at Jack, grinning. Jack seemed to have trouble collecting his thoughts.

"Well," he said, "glad everything worked out for you."

The boy nodded as he turned and went back to his own table with his two friends.

"You're a hero." Brandon clapped.

"Funny," Jack said, smirking. "Let's get back to Beefy. He wanted to show you fifty … what?"

"Fifty dollars. He had a fifty-dollar bill. He found it at the park." Will drummed his fingers on the table as he stared at Jack and Brandon. "And … he said he was going to get another on Friday night."

Their eyes widened.

"Fifty-dollar bills do not just pop up at the park," Brandon said. "The money must have come from the dealership's cash box. I think we should tell my father."

"So do I," Will agreed.

"Wait," Jack said as he paused with a finger in the air. "Maybe Friday night would be a good night to have a sleepover." He peered at Brandon.

"You mean follow him?" Brandon said. "Follow Boris Friday night and see where he goes?"

Jack nodded and they sought Will's approval.

"Brilliant." He gave them a fist bump as the bell rang to signal outdoor recess.

"C'mon, let's go grab a basketball court." Jack got up but paused when he noticed Will's feet. "Why are you wearing your old sneakers? Where are your new ones?"

Will shrugged. "I couldn't find them, which is why I was late today."

"Old sneakers are better anyway." Brandon stuck out his foot and wiggled his dirty-white hi-tops.

"*And* ..." Will grinned and took a step backwards. "... *I'm* going to play soccer today." He sprinted away as Jack took a good-natured swipe at him.

Chapter 12

"Where are you going?" Will asked Wendy Friday night, as she dropped her rain jacket and overstuffed sleeping bag by the front door.

"Sleepover at Kimberly's."

"Again?"

"Well, where are you going?"

"Sleepover at Brandon's."

"Again?"

Will had to admit she had a point.

"Ava's coming," Wendy said.

Will's stomach did a little flip. "Really?" He brushed some imaginary lint from his sleeve and dared not to look at her knowing his freckled cheeks were red.

"Yes, Kimberly invited her since she sits right behind her now, and we play soccer every day."

"Cool." Will turned to grab his bag by her feet and snuck a peek at Wendy. The merriment in her eyes told him he wasn't fooling her.

Mr. Abbott came through the door with pizza, and the family prayed and ate dinner together before the twins left.

"Stay alert and aware," Mrs. Abbott said, "and behave!"

"Yeah, Will, behave," Wendy said as they walked down the driveway.

"Us? We play video games and watch movies!"

"Oh, right! You go have fun then." Wendy stomped off toward Kimberly's house. Will laughed.

Ominous clouds gathered in the sky and rumbling thunder caused Will to pick up his pace as he headed toward Brandon's. He slowed when he saw a figure jogging in his direction. Ava!

"Hey!" He waved as she neared with a sleeping bag of her own. "Going to Kim's?"

"Yes. Going to Brandon's?"

"Yup."

Raindrops began to sprinkle and Ava gave a squeak and hurried on.

Will entered Brandon's house just when the downpour began. When Jack arrived, Brandon pushed his friends out of the living room.

"How are we supposed to do this in the rain?" Brandon asked, once they were out of earshot.

Jack reached into his overnight bag and pulled out a rain jacket. Brandon nodded, but Will frowned. Jack reached into his bag again and pulled out a second rain jacket, which he threw at Will.

"My brother won't mind if you borrow his."

The boys waited until dark to slip out. The rain drizzled and flashes of lightening sparked in the distance.

"I hope we catch him in the act," Will said. They hunched over and crept around the privet hedges in the neighborhood.

"Yeah, a little more info would have been helpful. 'Friday night at the park' is kind of vague," Jack said.

"Well, sorry! Next time Boris comes into my kitchen and shows me a fifty-dollar bill, I'll be sure to get more details," Will shot back.

"Sshhh." Brandon pulled the hood of his rain jacket up as the drizzle turned into a steady rain. Thunder rumbled. Will and Jack pulled up their hoods and they settled into a bushy area across the street from Boris's house where they could spy on him.

"He's not going out in this." Jack wiped his brow.

"Who's not going out in what?" they heard from behind.

Their shoulders drooped. They turned to find Kimberly, Wendy, and Ava decked out in rain jackets and boots, grinning at them.

"We knew you guys were up to someth—"

Jack pulled Wendy downward to hide her. Her friends ducked as a screen door slammed across the street and Boris charged out into the rain. He trotted toward the park with a blue bag slung over his shoulder.

"Please go home. Please." Will waved her off and the three boys snuck out of the bushes and followed Boris.

Boris jogged when the thunder rumbled and the rain poured down in torrents and he shielded the bag inside his jacket.

"I wonder what he's got in the bag?" Jack huffed as they jogged after him at a safe distance.

When they arrived, the boys ducked down behind the playground equipment and watched Boris enter the woods by the basketball court.

"Now what?" Jack said.

"We can't follow him," Brandon said. "He'll see us."

"We have to get closer. Come on." Will led the way as they sprinted out from behind the jungle gym and over to the slide. Crouching down, they peered through the rainy darkness into the woods trying to see some sign of Boris.

Will heard his sister's voice again, "Why are you guys following Boris?"

Words exploded from Jack's mouth through gritted teeth, "Why do you keep following us?"

"Get down," Brandon hissed. Everyone tried to squeeze together as Boris bolted from the woods and ran down the street.

"Wow! Did you see the look on his face?" Flickers of light reflected from Brandon's wide-eyed gaze.

"Terrified," Jack said. "And I noticed something else, too ..."

Will nodded. "He didn't have the bag anymore."

Chapter 13

Will sat at the kitchen table for breakfast on Sunday morning oblivious to Wendy as she snuck into the chair next to his.

"Wendy?" Mrs. Abbott's eyes narrowed.

"What?"

"You are not wearing those shorts to church."

"But, Mom, the picnic is today!"

"You can bring them and change afterward if you want."

"Fine—I'll just wear something else!" Wendy stomped back upstairs.

Will and his father shoveled spoonsful of cereal into their mouths with one hand while the other shielded their brows from the battle.

"When you get out of Sunday School, head over to the church field. Mrs. Bobrick and I will have the picnic set up," Mrs. Abbott said.

Will nodded, excited for the first day of Sunday School. All his friends were in the class, plus Kenny and Rob from the soccer team who went to Maple Grove Middle School. Will patted his pocket to make sure his lucky stone was there. He wanted to show Kenny, who had his own rock collection. Will felt the twenty-dollar bill in his pocket too and sighed. He had been thinking about putting the money toward a new pair of soccer cleats, but his mom hadn't noticed he lost his new sneakers yet. When she did, he knew she would make him buy a new pair.

Beautiful early fall weather had replaced the storminess of the last two days, and there were friendly greetings all around as the parishioners arrived at church. Wendy stood outside with Father Anthony, holding a beautiful collection jar she had painted for the Clean Water Fund, which they had started for the African village.

Will noticed a teenage girl with tight red curls talking to Wendy and Father Anthony. The girl broke into a huge smile, and she reached into her pocket for a donation. She dropped some bills into the large jar Wendy held and ran to catch up with a tall dark-haired man talking to Mr. Lang. This drive will be a success with Wendy involved, Will thought, proud of his twin.

After mass, the kids walked to their assigned Sunday School classrooms.

Jack grumbled, "Who's the teacher gonna be?"

"Hopefully not someone's grandpa like we had in fifth grade," Samantha said.

"Remember when Boris stole his reading glasses and we didn't do anything for that whole class?" Kim giggled.

Boris heard his name. "What?"

"Nothing, Boris," Brandon said.

"Why are you talking about me? I heard you—"

Jack turned. "What are you, paranoid or something?"

Boris balled his fists, and Jack, chest out, stepped up to the challenge.

Will grabbed Jack and nodded toward the front of the classroom where Knobby was standing. He was out of uniform, in his street clothes.

"Looking sharp, Knobby!"

"Are you our teacher?"

"No, no, no-o-o-o," Knobby held up his hands and backed slowly out of the room, grinning.

"Surprise!" Miss Chapman smiled from her seat behind the desk. "I have you guys, again."

The classmates responded.

"You got us?"

"We got you, again?"

"Thank God."

"Yes!"

"Well, I'm glad we're all happy." Miss Chapman said. "This is your last year of Sunday School. As eighth graders, I want to send you off with all the tools you'll need as you go forward." She held up a workbook. "Our first topic will be the Ten Commandments."

Kimberly raised her hand. "But the Ten Commandments aren't tools. They're just a list of things we're supposed to do."

"But they are tools, Kim. A tool is something you use. You can use the commandments to help you choose between right and wrong. So, you will each pick a commandment to study."

"Okay, I'll do the one about lying," Kenny said.

"You picked the easiest one," Jack barked. "I'll do the stealing one.

Miss Chapman held up her hand. "We'll do this fairly. You will each pick a number from one to ten, which will match a commandment number."

"But our class has fourteen people," Wendy said.

Boris raised his hand. "I know what we can do. Let's make up four more commandments. Thou shalt not—"

"Boris!" Miss Chapman frowned. "Some of you will have to double up on a commandment." She cut fourteen squares of paper, jotted numbers on them and put them into an empty flowerpot. "Okay, pick."

Will waited his turn as Miss Chapman moved around the room.

"I got number six." Kimberly held up her paper.

"I got four," Rob said.

Will watched Ava look at the number she picked. She glanced at him and held up two fingers.

"I got four too." Brandon said. He fist-bumped Rob.

Boris stuck his hand in the pot and pulled out a paper. "Five!" he said, waving his pick in the air.

Will's turn. He reached in and grabbed a number. His stomach flipped when he saw the number two. He glanced over at Ava, and nodded with a smile, but his expression fell when he saw Wendy had the same number as Boris. He sighed and leaned over to switch with her, but Derek was quicker. Derek grabbed her five and slipped her his eight.

Miss Chapman noted everyone's commandment number. After her lecture, she dismissed the class. They ran to the field to join the church picnic.

Will watched Boris who stood off from the group checking the time.

"I'll make room, Boris," Samantha waved him over and scooted closer to Ava to create more space in the circle.

Boris checked the time again. "Nah, I gotta go." He lumbered off. Will exchanged a look with Brandon and Jack. He wished they could follow him. Instead, they challenged the seventh-grade class to a soccer game.

Later, Will sought Derek. He saw him leaving and jogged over. "Good game." Will put his fist out and got a bump. "And … thanks for switching numbers with Wendy." Derek shrugged. "Um, we have our first soccer practice tomorrow night at the park. The Tigers could use a couple more players."

Mrs. Harrison beeped the horn, and Derek headed toward his car. "What time?"

"Six-thirty. Cleats and a water bottle … and shin guards!" Will called. He walked to the car where his mother waited with Wendy. *I wish I knew what Boris was up to—and I forgot to show Kenny my lucky stone.*

Chapter 14

"Please welcome the new student. Her name is Betsy. She's from Los Angeles. Take out your science book."

Mr. Lockwood's class craned their necks to study the new girl. Betsy, grinning ear to ear, strode to an empty desk in the back of the room, red curls bouncing.

"I met her at church yesterday." Wendy leaned toward Will. "She's really nice."

"Look at Jack." Will chuckled.

Jack, who sat near Betsy, hung onto her every word as she and another girl chatted. Then, after jumping into their conversation, he blushed when Betsy laughed at his comments.

When lunchtime came, Will saw the girls whisk Betsy away to their table to endure a lively interrogation. The boys couldn't hear much over the cafeteria din, but the word tattoo did drift over to them, followed by giggling.

"My dad knows them—Betsy's family," Brandon said. "He was talking to them at church yesterday. She lives with her uncle."

Jack frowned. "Why?"

Brandon shrugged.

"Why'd they move here?"

"You mean move back," Brandon said. "Her uncle grew up here. My dad went to school with him."

Will tilted his head. Something about this story sounds familiar, he thought.

"I didn't hear everything they were talking about yesterday," Brandon glanced over at the girls, "but I overheard her uncle say 'Mayfield' and 'tragedy.'"

"Whoa—Mayfield?" Jack asked. "As in the old Mayfield mansion?"

"Yes!" Will banged a fist on the table. He looked around and lowered his voice. "Do you know who she is? She's the survivor of the fire at the Jamison house." He told them about his conversation with Mrs. Larson.

"How did she get out?" Jack asked.

"No one knows."

The bell rang for recess, and Will rose from the table. He saw Derek nudge Jack and point toward Lucas Coleman's feet. Jack's expression changed to fury and he pounced on Lucas.

"What are you doing?" Lucas struggled to push Jack away.

"Those are Will's sneakers!" Jack pushed Lucas up against the table where the girls sat, sending chairs flying. The girls squealed and ran as a melee broke out, knocking Betsy down.

Will rushed over to help Brandon separate Lucas and Jack but found himself face to face with Boris. Boris sneered and shoved Will to the floor. From his vantage point, Will had a perfect view of his own sneakers—on Lucas Coleman's feet. Mr. Lockwood hauled Will up and marched him down to Principal Thomas's office, along with Brandon, Jack, Boris, and Lucas.

Principal Thomas furrowed his brow and shook his head at each of them. "What was that all about?"

Will's face was still flushed. He pointed at Lucas. "He's wearing my sneakers."

Jack chimed in. "He stole them!"

"No, they're mine! I found them." Lucas shot back a searing glare.

Brandon rose. "Yeah, right!"

Principal Thomas held up his hand. "Will, why do you think those are your sneakers?"

"I can just tell."

"I'll need more proof."

Will sat back in his seat and tried to calm himself. "My initials are inside."

Lucas untied and yanked off the left sneaker. He looked inside and handed it to Principal Thomas.

"Under the tongue," Will said.

Principal Thomas lifted the tongue. "W-A," he confirmed, showing the initials for all the boys to see.

Lucas scoffed and glared at Boris, who smirked. He pulled the other sneaker off and threw it to the ground. "I found them in the woods. I didn't know they were his. Can I go get my other sneakers out of my gym locker?"

Principal Thomas looked at Will.

Will shrugged, "Fine, let him go."

"I'll just buy my own pair." Lucas flashed a fifty-dollar bill at them and stomped out, followed by Boris. Principal Thomas closed the door, but the boys heard Lucas hollering at Boris.

"How did your sneakers end up in the woods, Will?" Principal Thomas stared at him.

Will stood silent for a moment. He looked at Jack and Brandon. "I don't know," he said.

After Principal Thomas dismissed them, Will and his friends went outside. Mr. Lockwood eyed them from his recess monitor post.

Brandon sat and plucked at the grass. "How did he get your sneakers?"

"I don't know ... good thing Derek even noticed."

"Yeah." Brandon looked at Jack. "Will and I had to hold you back, Terrier. You have to deal with your anger issues."

Will nodded. "Another question is, where did Lucas get a fifty-dollar bill?" He saw Wendy wave and they joined her along with Ava and Kimberly who had linked arms with Betsy.

"Did you get detention? Mom will be furious."

Jack answered for him. "No, but he got his sneakers back." He zeroed in on Betsy. "Are you okay? Sorry you got knocked over. Not a great way to start a new school." Everyone stared at him, slack-jawed. "What? It's true."

Betsy smiled at him and waved away the concern. "I forgive you. I'm made of pretty tough stuff."

Derek jogged over to join them and stared at Will's feet. "What happened?"

"Got 'em back. Thanks for the heads up. Lucas said he found them in the woods."

Derek's eyebrows shot up. "Lucas is pretty mad. He told Boris to 'keep his stupid money' and threw cash at him."

"Boris is making new friends everywhere." Brandon gestured toward the teacher's parking lot where Boris exchanged words with Micky O'Brien.

Will squinted. "Boris is involved in this somehow. I just don't know how."

Chapter 15

On the way home, Will and his friends stopped to pet Petunia who was out for an afternoon stroll with Mrs. Larson.

"Any word on the robbery at the dealership, Brandon?"

"No, but my dad is hopeful the insurance will cover most of the damage."

Mrs. Larson shook her head. "Haven't had a robbery around here in a long time ... strange. Well, anyway, bring Buster over for a playdate soon, Will. Petunia misses him."

As they left, Jack gaped at Will. "Why didn't you ask her about the new girl?"

"I was going to ... but I didn't know how to bring the subject up."

The boys parted ways with Brandon in his driveway.

"Soccer tonight," Will reminded him. "And my mother wants to have a pizza party at Pie Place on Friday."

"Ahh, the big birthday—thirteen on the thirteenth! So ... did you invite Derek?" When Will nodded, Brandon laughed as he went inside, "Ha! I told you he was an okay guy!"

When they reached the Abbott's house, Jack cleared his throat. "So, uh, maybe Wendy can ask Betsy to come to the pizza party."

Will glanced sideways at him and got punched.

Will went inside and heard Wendy in the kitchen.

"... and she's from Los Angeles. She doesn't have her ears double pierced, but she wants a tattoo."

"Don't you even …" Mrs. Abbott warned, laughing. "Hi, honey," she said to Will. "Wendy was just telling me about the new girl in your class."

"Yeah—Betsy." He headed straight to the pantry and searched for a snack. "Brandon said she lives with her uncle. Mr. Lang went to school with him."

"Why does she live with her uncle?" Wendy asked.

Will turned to his mother. "You probably know him. Didn't you go to school with Mr. Lang too?"

"Is her last name Jamison?"

"I think so," Will said.

"Yes—I saw her name on her lunch bag," Wendy said. "Why?" She looked between her mother and Will. "Wait—do you mean that Jamison? Whose house burned down? Is she the baby …?"

"It sounds like she may be." Mrs. Abbott paused. "Why don't you invite her to the pizza party Friday night? And Will, I'm glad to see you found your sneakers."

"How did you know they were lost?"

"You weren't wearing them, so I just figured …" Mrs. Abbot opened the refrigerator. "Dinner is early tonight. You both have soccer, and I have 'Meet the Teacher Night' at school." She pulled out the burger meat to create patties. "Unfortunately, your teacher won't even be there. I'm disappointed, but apparently he has a second job, so Principal Thomas will be filling in." She fashioned the lumps into patties and wrapped them in cellophane. "So, why don't you get right to your homework."

"Mr. Lockwood doesn't give homework," Wendy said.

"… or tests." Will smiled.

"Are you sure?"

"No, but he never mentions them."

"Well, maybe I'll mention them tonight."

Chapter 16

Will rode to the park early and dropped his bike near the benches. He finished lacing his cleats and started kicking the ball around with Kenny.

"Wait—check out this rock I found," Will said and ran back to his bag.

Kenny weighed the stone in his hand and probed it like an expert. "Great crystals."

"Yeah, they make a pattern of the letter L."

Kenny held the stone up to the fading sunlight "That's not an L. That's a T." He flipped the stone over and positioned it just right, and Will could see that the bottom line of the L was actually longer than he thought, forming a T pattern.

"T for Tigers!" Kenny tossed the stone back and ran over to where Coach Jeffries was initiating warm up stretches, leaving Will angling the stone to marvel at the T.

Stones aren't lucky anyway, he thought and stuck his rock back in his bag.

The team played for an hour. Exhausted, the boys flopped down on the grass with their water bottles.

From his spot, Will had a perfect view of the playground. The woods! Suddenly, things were starting to make sense. Will jumped up. His teammates were leaving, and he looked to grab Brandon and Jack, but instead came face to face with Wendy and Ava.

"Our team is finished too." Wendy waved to Derek who sat in his mom's car. "Want to ride home together?"

"Uh … sure, but we're making a pitstop first." Will said.

Jack and Brandon approached. "What's up?"

"Follow me." Will outlined his theory and rushed them to the wooded passage Boris had entered a few nights before.

"Wait. You think Boris had your sneakers in the bag he left in the woods Friday night?" Jack's brow creased with doubt. "How could he get them?"

"He was at my house, remember? Then I couldn't find them the next day. And where did Lucas say he found the sneakers?"

"The woods …" Jack kicked an acorn.

Wendy dug her heels in at the entrance. "I'm not going in," she said. "The forest is way too dark."

Brandon, the only one with a cell phone, turned on the flashlight. "Don't be chicken. Come on."

Will sighed. *I have to start remembering a flashlight.*

Brandon shined the light around. With no clear path visible, they could not tell which direction Boris had taken, and the darkness increased around them by the minute.

"We'll have to split up," Jack said.

"Are you crazy?" Wendy squeaked and hunched her shoulders.

"I'm with her." Ava tugged Wendy's jacket. "Plus, we only have one light."

"Well, he wasn't in here long, so he couldn't have gone too far," Will said. "Let's go straight."

With Brandon leading the way, they pushed forward. Will listened carefully, mindful of Boris's terrified flight, but he could hear nothing above the chirping of the late season cicadas.

Wendy muttered, "What are we looking for anyway?"

"I don't know exactly," Will said, "but I'll know when I see it."

"I think I see something." Brandon shined the light on a wooden box nailed to a tree.

"Looks like a bat box," Ava said. Wendy groaned.

Jack climbed a couple of feet up the tree and peeked in. "Relax, the box is empty."

"Uh, okay, well … what's hanging next to the box?"

Brandon moved the beam of light slightly, and they gasped. A blue plastic bag, now empty, hung from a branch.

"Just what I thought!" Will crossed his arms across his chest. "The bag Beefy carried in here Friday night looked identical."

"C'mon," Wendy said. "Let's get out of here."

Will took one last look at the blue bag hanging next to the bat box and followed the group out to the playground.

"Okay, I have about a million questions about this," Brandon said as they walked back to their bikes. "There is no way Lucas found your sneakers here by accident."

Will thought about the heated exchange between Lucas and Boris outside of Principal Thomas's office. "Boris led him here."

"But why?" Ava asked.

Will stopped. "I think someone paid him fifty-dollars to do it."

Chapter 17

On Friday morning Will heard a knock on his bedroom door.

Wendy peeked in. "Happy Birthday!"

"Happy Birthday." He yawned and sat up.

She came in and sat at the edge of his bed. "We're teenagers now. I don't feel any different. Do you?"

Will tapped himself from his head to his shoulders and elbows. "Nope, I feel the same."

Wendy threw a pillow at him.

They went downstairs to eat a birthday breakfast. Chocolate chip pancakes for Will. Blueberry for Wendy.

Their father was already at the kitchen table enjoying a plate of both. "Boy, I love your birthday. Happy birthday, guys!"

Their mother kissed them and placed two small identically wrapped boxes on the table in front of them. "Happy birthday from Dad and me—a gift fit for teenagers." Will reached for his, but then Mrs. Abbott moved the box out of the way. "Uh-uh, not 'til your party tonight." The twins groaned at their mother and dug into their pancakes. "Make sure your friends arrive at Pie Place at six o'clock sharp. And that reminds me—Jack's parents are going out of town, so he'll stay here for the weekend."

"Cool," Will said.

Jack waited outside for them. "The temperature will be about a zillion degrees today. Oh, and happy birthday."

As they walked through the neighborhood, they picked up Brandon and Kimberly.

"I can't wait until tonight," Wendy said. "I wonder what my parents got me."

"Earrings?" Kim tugged Wendy's ear. "Your mother knows you want your ears double pierced."

"Not unless Will got earrings too." Wendy laughed. "The boxes my mom put on the table this morning were the same."

"Can we go over the plan for tonight again?" Jack said.

Brandon leaned in as Will explained. "After Pie Place, we wait till most of the kids have left. Then we say we are going to the park for a little while."

"Will your mom mind if we hang out after dark?" Kimberly looked at Wendy.

"I don't think so. We are thirteen, after all."

Will wiped sweat from his brow. "Then we can stake out different areas around the playground and wait to see if Beefy shows up."

"And if he does, we jump him." Jack finished, slapping his hand on his thigh.

"Don't be stupid." Brandon punched him. "We have to catch him doing something first. There's no law against going to the park."

"Fine." Jack glanced at Wendy. "Are you sure Betsy can come?"

"Yes," she said, making a kissy face and scooting out of arm's reach, laughing.

Upon hearing Will and Wendy's birthday wishes, Mr. Lockwood broke from his usual impersonal demeanor to comment, "Thirteen on Friday the Thirteenth? Rather unlucky, eh?"

Boris leaned over Will's shoulder and whispered loud enough for Wendy to hear. "The date's not unlucky when you're getting another fifty bucks."

Will shrugged him off. "The date's not unlucky, anyway. It's just a dumb superstition."

"And I don't care how much money you have, Boris," Wendy said, "but maybe you should put some in the Clean Water Fund jar."

Boris sat back, rejecting the suggestion with a snicker.

The afternoon heat suspended the recess soccer game, but not the basketball. "Come on," Jack called from the court, ball on hip, to the group sitting under a shady tree.

"He's not going to leave us alone," Brandon groaned.

"Fine," Will sighed, dragging himself up. "Anyone else? Derek?"

"Sure." Derek rose.

Betsy jumped up. "I'll play."

"Okay, we need one more. Where's Micky?" Will looked around. Brandon nudged him and nodded over toward the side of the building where Micky and Boris were deep in conversation.

As the classes trudged in from recess, hot and sweaty, Will found Micky O'Brien.

"Why weren't you on the basketball court today? We could have used you."

"Too hot," Micky grunted and mumbled something Will couldn't quite make out.

"What?"

"I said I can't go to your party later. Sorry." Micky avoided looking at Will.

"Sure, no problem." Will shrugged. Micky ran ahead.

"What's wrong?" Ava came up behind Will.

"I wonder why Micky's been spending so much time with Boris."

"I agree," she said.

At six o'clock sharp, Will, Wendy, and their friends gathered at Pie Place for the birthday celebration.

Wendy introduced Betsy to her parents.

Mrs. Abbott shook Betsy's hand. "I'm very happy to meet you, Betsy. I hope you are settling in nicely."

"Yes, I am, thank you."

"I think I know your Uncle Jerry. We went to school here in Fern Valley together."

Betsy's face lit up. "I'll tell him."

Finally, stuffed with pizza, they gathered around to watch Will and Wendy open their birthday presents. They opened everyone's gifts and saved their parent's gifts for last. Mr. Abbott brought out the two gifts which had been on the kitchen table that morning. "Here you go, guys!" He stepped back, grinning as they tore the paper off.

"Cell phones!" Will's mouth dropped open. When he glanced at Wendy, he was sure that all thoughts of earrings had banished when she saw hers. Everyone gathered around to gawk at the sleek new phones.

"I know I told you that you'd have to wait until high school, but ..." Mrs. Abbott's voice trailed off. Will knew immediately what she didn't want to say—that recent concerns drove her to break her own rule.

"This is great, Mom! Thanks, Dad!"

As the group sang, Will tried to think of a wish, but the only thing that popped into his head was Boris. He really didn't want to waste a birthday wish on Boris.

Wendy blew her candles out. Then closing his eyes, Will blew out his candles and prayed that tonight at the park he would find out what Boris was up to.

Chapter 18

"Wow, I'm so glad our parents are letting us go to the park," Wendy said. "I wasn't sure they would."

"Maybe because we all live close enough to the park to walk home," Kimberly said. "—except for you, Derek."

"Yeah, dude, you should have brought a bike," Brandon said.

"I'm not worried. I'll just jog." Derek looked at Betsy. "How far are you?"

"Yeah, Betsy—we don't even know where you live," Wendy said.

"Oh, not too far." Betsy waved in no particular direction. "My uncle is renting a house."

Will kicked a stone in the polite silence that followed.

"My family did own a house here, but ..."

"We know about the fire, Betsy." Wendy squeezed Betsy's hand. Everyone nodded. "It's so sad ... I'm sorry."

"Thanks—and Uncle Jerry's great." She smiled. "So, why are we staking out this particular spot?"

Everyone waited for Will. "If Beefy took my sneakers, and if they were in the blue bag, and if Lucas really found them in the woods, then I think the transfer happened here."

"That's a lot of ifs, buddy," Jack shook his head as they passed the soccer field.

"And you heard Boris say he was getting another fifty dollars tonight, right?"

Wendy nodded. "Yes, Ava. I even heard him, too."

When they reached a split pathway, they separated into pairs and started walking toward different sections of the playground.

"Wait! How will we communicate if we see something?" Kimberly asked.

Will tapped his new cell phone. "We can text each other."

"Problem." Jack stood with Betsy, who shrugged. "We don't have one."

"But I can whistle." Betsy cupped her hands around her pursed lips and let out a musical warble, delighting the group.

"Wow—okay, if we see something," Jack pointed to Betsy, "she'll do that."

Will and Ava, having chosen the corner closest to the woods, positioned themselves under the slide where they could spy on Boris. Brandon and Kim were crouched down behind the merry-go-round and Derek and Wendy tried to stay out of sight behind the bars of the jungle gym.

Darkness settled in as Will looked around. "I don't see Jack and Betsy," he whispered. Ava scanned the playground. She finally pointed to the far corner and then raised her finger a little higher. Will snickered when he saw they had climbed a leafy tree and were watching from a few feet off the ground.

"Look at the bats," Ava said. Will followed her gaze up to where the small black creatures were darting about, dipping and diving among each other. "They come out at this time of night to catch bugs."

"Pretty cool," Will said.

"Do you really think he'll come?"

Will nodded. "He said something about Friday the thirteenth not being unlucky and getting another fifty bucks."

"I don't think this day is unlucky anyway," Ava said. "I don't believe in superstitions."

"Me either." Will reached into his pocket and pulled his stone out. "I used to think this was a lucky stone." He handed it to her. "The crystal pattern on the face looked like an L, for lucky. But then, Kenny showed me the L was really a T."

Ava held the stone up but could not see the crystals in the evening dusk. "So why do you still keep this?" She handed his stone back.

"I don't know. I was going to add it to my rock collection." He shrugged. "I guess I sound stupid." He went to toss the stone into the woodchips, but Ava grabbed it.

"Don't. You don't sound stupid at all. Can I keep it?"

Will nodded. His heart flipped as she slipped the stone into her pocket.

Suddenly, Will's phone vibrated and he saw a text.

Brandon: He's coming right toward you.

Will's stomach lurched as they heard approaching footsteps, and they tried to make themselves as small as possible behind the slide. He held his own breath and frantically tried to think of a good excuse in case Boris caught him and Ava hiding together. There wasn't one. He knew Boris would draw the wrong conclusion, and Will would not be able to tell him the truth.

Then to Will's horror, Boris sat on the edge of the slide. "Creepy bats," Will heard him mutter, and out of the corner of his eye he saw a rock fly. Ava twitched, and Will shook his head at her. They heard a bag rustle and drop with a metallic thud. Boris started grabbing rocks and throwing them in the air with both fists. Will focused on the bag laying a few feet from him but could not tell what was inside.

Boris picked up the bag and paced. Will started to sweat. With only a turn of his head, Boris would see them. Suddenly, a shrill whistle came from the trees on the far side of the playground. Boris froze and listened. Another whistle sounded.

"What the—" Boris began trotting across the woodchips straight toward the merry-go-round where Brandon and Kim were hiding.

"Yo, Boris." Will heard Derek's voice and peeked out. Derek stood near the sidewalk, trying to draw Boris away from the merry-go-round.

Boris turned to him. "What are you doing here, Harrison?"

"Just walking home from town."

"Long walk."

Boris walked toward Derek. Will saw Brandon and Kimberly dart from behind the merry-go-round to the safety of the trees by Betsy and Jack.

"Well, what are you doing here?"

"A job, Harrison." Boris shot back. Will saw him shift the bag from one hand to the other. "None of your business. Just keep walking."

Derek shrugged and sauntered off. Boris returned to pacing. Will was beginning to think he and Ava might be stranded under the slide all night. Finally, Boris kicked some stones and stomped into the woods.

Will texted Brandon and Wendy, "Let's get out of here."

He poked his head out—and then ducked and held Ava back. Coming right toward them was Micky O'Brien. Micky stopped near the slide and looked around.

"O'Brien!" Boris beckoned from the wooded entrance and Micky ran in.

"Unbelievable," Brandon had texted.

"I'm going to find Derek." Wendy answered and they saw her sprint out from behind the jungle gym and head down the street.

"Come on." Ava tugged at Will's arm but froze as Boris and Micky jogged out of the woods and slowed within earshot.

"Th-th-that was weird." Micky said. "Who put the note in the box?"

"Who knows," Boris growled and shoved the bag he was holding into Micky's hands. "I did what my note says." He crumpled and tossed a piece of paper onto the ground. "Now just do what your note says, and you'll get one of these!" He waved a fifty-dollar bill at Micky and ran off.

Will slid out a little farther just in time to see Micky's perplexed expression when he read his note. Then he left.

Will and his friends jumped out to grab the crumpled note Boris had tossed to the ground. Will flattened out the paper so they all could read the five words scrawled in black ink.

GIVE THE CAN TO MICKY

Chapter 19

Will woke early on Sunday morning. He tiptoed past Jack, who slept curled up on an air mattress, and past Brandon, still snoring and sprawled across his sleeping bag. They had stayed up late watching a movie after spending Saturday afternoon, at Will's insistence, searching for clues in the woods but finding none.

Will headed downstairs. When he entered the kitchen, he was surprised to see his dad already awake and at his computer, a steaming mug of coffee in hand.

"Work on Sunday?"

Mr. Abbott sighed. "I have to put in a claim for a client who had a fender bender last night." He closed his laptop and slipped it into his bag. "I've been meaning to ask you something." He spoke in hushed tones. "Mr. Bobrick stopped by my office the other day to pay a bill."

"Yeah?" Will's heart thudded in his chest and he tried to look nonchalant as he reached across the counter for a banana.

"He said Boris seems to have a lot of money lately, and he's not sure where he's getting the cash from."

"Did he ask him, Dad?"

"Yes, but he was vague. So, I was wondering if you knew anything."

Will wasn't sure how to answer honestly. "Dad, Boris is ... complicated."

Mr. Abbott nodded. "Well, his father is worried."

With good reason, Will thought.

He jogged back upstairs to wake Jack and Brandon. After breakfast, they piled into the car with the rest of the Abbotts and headed to St. Therese's.

A small crowd gathered on the side of the church when they pulled into the parking lot.

"Let's go, kids. I want to get a seat," Mrs. Abbott said.

"We're coming … save us one."

Wendy, Will, Brandon, and Jack bypassed the entrance and turned the corner of the brick building to see what the crowd gawked at. They froze when they saw the word spray-painted on the side of the church building.

T E R R I E R

"Oh, no," Will gasped.

"I'm gonna throw up," Jack said. Wendy put an arm around him.

"Relax," Brandon whispered, looking around. "No one knows your nickname."

Will knew Brandon was just trying to make Jack feel better because—everyone knew his nickname. Everyone who knew Jack anyway. They walked into the church, conscious of some disapproving stares, and slid into their pew. Mrs. Abbott smiled at them, oblivious to the graffiti on the side of the church building.

Will thought maybe Father Anthony didn't know yet. He gave his usual upbeat sermon followed by an encouraging update on the Clean Water Fund collection. When they tried to slip by unnoticed after mass, he greeted them and pumped each of their hands.

"Wendy, I think your jar for the collection is helping." His expression beamed.

"That's really great, Father." Wendy nodded as the boys scooted away. "Well, I don't want to be late for Sunday School … see you next week." And she hurried after them.

"Everyone is gonna think I spray-painted the church," Jack seethed. He stopped outside the classroom and tried to get control of his anger.

"Well, you didn't. Only a few people saw the graffiti," Brandon nodded as he put his hands on his hips.

"Yeah, and if we can clean the paint off the wall somehow, no one else will know," Will stuck his hands in his pockets. "Let's go to the hardware store after Sunday School for supplies."

The plan fell apart when they entered the classroom. Officer Knobby waited in uniform. He stood next to Miss Chapman who clasped her hands in a ball under her chin. Will, Jack, Brandon, and Wendy waved hello with a half-smile and took their seats.

"What's up ... Terrier," Boris said as everyone turned to the sound of his voice.

Before Jack had time to react, Knobby called him.

"Jack, can I talk to you outside a minute?"

Will leaned in. "Don't forget, you're innocent."

Jack stood tall and left the room.

Chapter 20

Watching Officer Knobby walk out with Jack, Miss Chapman prayed before jumping into the lesson.

"Last week everyone was assigned one of the Ten Commandments. I did ask you to think about your commandment ..."

Will stared out the window as his teacher's voice lulled in the background. He snapped to attention when Miss Chapman, glancing at the classroom door, said, "I'm not sure which commandment Jack had ..."

Boris snickered. "The one that says, 'Thou shall not write on the—'"

"Boris!" Miss Chapman pointed her finger at him before continuing. "If you have the same commandment as someone else, you can choose to work on your own project or work together."

Wendy raised her hand. "Can Betsy work with me? She wasn't here last week."

Miss Chapman nodded and introduced Betsy to the class. "You may get started."

"I'm doin' my own, Harrison," Boris bellowed from across the room. Derek shrugged. Will and Ava, with the same thought in mind, moved their desks closer together.

A low, pleasant chatter filled the room as everyone worked. Will kept glancing at the door, waiting for Jack to return as he and Ava worked on a presentation promoting respect for God's holy name. He started to worry Jack might actually be in trouble when Knobby opened the door and leaned in.

"Will and Brandon, can I see you a moment."

They went out into the hall and followed Knobby to an empty classroom where Jack sat slumped in a chair. He shook his head when his friends entered.

"I know Jack is not responsible for the graffiti on the side of the church." Knobby pointed to the projection screen. "We have video from the church security camera of the perpetrator who is clearly not Jack. But I do need to verify his whereabouts last night."

"He was at my house all night," Will said. "You can even ask my parents." Brandon nodded.

Knobby shrugged. "Is Jack having issues with anyone who would want to frame him for this?"

"No." Jack crossed his arms over his chest. His friends shook their heads.

"Okay then, last question." Knobby pressed play and an image appeared on the screen. "Do you recognize this person?"

The boys stared at the dark and grainy image of a hooded person dressed in black who spray-painted the seven letters on the wall before exiting from view. Will glanced at Jack. To anyone else his expression was unreadable, but Will could see fury in his eyes.

Knobby stopped the video and waited for the boys to respond. "Well?"

Beads of sweat formed on Will's brow. Brandon squirmed.

Only Jack remained cool under Knobby's gaze. "No, sir."

Brandon agreed with a shake of his head. Will followed—glancing down at his shoes—knowing they did recognize the unmistakable form of Micky O'Brien.

Chapter 21

"Where's your fifty dollars—huh, Micky?" Jack shoved Micky against a fence where Jack, Brandon, and Will had waylaid him on his way to school Monday morning.

"What?" Micky, taller and stronger, darted his gaze back and forth between the boys, and trembled.

"Empty your pockets!"

Micky looked at Will, who nodded. He dropped his backpack and put both hands in his front pockets and turned them inside out. Empty. "I don't know what—"

"Yes, you do know, Micky," Brandon said. "We know you sprayed the church wall—for money!"

Jack shoved him again. "What's wrong with you? I thought we were friends!"

"We are—it wasn't me. I don't know what you're talking about!"

Jack noticed Micky's tears welling up and backed off.

"Hey, what's going on here?" An elderly man wheeling his garbage can down his driveway, neared. He focused on Micky. "Are you okay, son?"

Micky didn't answer. He grabbed his backpack, backed away, and ran off. The old man's eyes narrowed and his lips tightened as he glared at Will, Brandon, and Jack.

Will waved. "Just a misunderstanding, sir. Sorry we disturbed you." The boys turned away and scuttled around the corner.

"So much for the sneak attack." Jack kicked some stones.

"I really thought if we caught him off guard, he'd confess," Will said as they plodded toward school. "I do not want to end up in Principal Thomas's office again."

"We really should confront Boris," Brandon said. "I bet he's the one with the dealership's stolen money."

"No, I don't think so. I think the person who wrote this note has the money." Will pulled the crumpled note out of his pocket and they stared at the words again: GIVE THE CAN TO MICKY. "Look, if we confront Boris, we might spook him. Then he'll quit 'his job' and we'll never find out who's behind this note."

Brandon sighed and nodded. "Come on, we're gonna be late."

They arrived to join their class walking in and headed to their desks. Boris followed Micky to his seat.

"Can you see Micky's desk?" Will whispered to Wendy. "What are they doing?"

Wendy craned her neck. "I can't see."

Will caught Brandon's attention and motioned toward Micky's desk. "What are they doing?" Brandon looked over, and Will saw his eyes widen.

"Good morning. Take out your math books. Boris, go to your own seat," Mr. Lockwood said.

Boris strutted across the room.

"Wendy," Boris whispered as he crept past. "Like my new sneakers?"

Wendy ignored him. Will tried not to look but couldn't help himself. Boris wore a new pair of sneakers identical to Will's. He plopped himself into his seat, sighing through a mischievous grin. Will shook his head, glanced around the classroom, and then noticed Ava smiling at him.

"I like yours better," she mouthed. Will grinned on one side of his mouth and turned, staring at his desk.

All morning Will saw Brandon glancing at him and could tell he was busting with news. He wished he had his cell phone. A quick text would have been handy, but his mom had held her ground. "No phones in school until next year."

"I saw the money!" Brandon stood with his hands flat on the lunch table. "Micky has the fifty dollars!"

"Shh!" Will glanced around at the other tables.

Jack's face grew red. "What? How? He didn't this morning."

"No … I saw him pull an envelope with money out of his desk," Brandon said. "I think … maybe Boris planted the cash for him before he arrived."

"No," Will shook his head, "someone else did. We have to find out who wrote the note we found at the park." They gazed across the room at Micky who sat at a table alone. "This is stupid. I'm just gonna go talk to him."

"Wait." Brandon held his arm. "Look." Derek pulled a chair over to sit with Micky just as the bell rang for recess.

"Come on," Wendy said, "we're all playing soccer today."

Will and his friends played, but he kept watching the exit door to see if Derek and Micky came out. Finally, as the game ended, they saw Derek.

Jack held his hands up as Derek approached. "Where's Micky?"

"He went home sick. I was at the nurse's office with him this whole time."

"Well, what did he say?" Brandon picked up the soccer ball.

"He said to give this to Jack … " Derek pulled a neatly folded piece of paper out of his pocket, " … and that he wanted to forget the whole 'creepy' thing. I tried to get more out of him, but he clammed up."

The group crowded around as Jack unfolded the paper. A fifty-dollar bill slipped out and fluttered to the ground. Will scooped the money up and Jack held the paper out for them to see.

SORRY

"So, I'm supposed to forget what happened?" Jack furrowed his brow.

"Yes," Betsy said.

"And what do I do about the fifty?" He pointed to the money Will held.

"We could give the money back to Mr. Lang—if we knew for sure the fifty was from his cash box."

"Check it out." Derek nodded toward the side of the building where Boris stood face to face with Richie Tan.

Will thrust his hands upward. "Unbelievable!" He walked toward them, until he heard Mr. Lockwood's voice.

"Did you not hear the bell ring, Mr. Abbott?"

"Uh, no … I didn't …" Will saw all the kids still enjoying recess. "I don't think—" Rrrrring! Mr. Lockwood turned and walked away, leaving the boys frustrated.

"We can talk to Richie tonight at practice," Brandon said. Will nodded.

Will kicked a ball to Stuart. "Where's Richie?"

Stuart shrugged. He tapped the ball back to Will. "He told me after school he couldn't come tonight."

Will clenched his teeth and took a shot that sailed past the goal to the edge of the playground. As he jogged over to retrieve the ball, he glanced at the woods. I should take another look in there—after practice, he thought.

Will waited until most of the teams had left. "Okay," he said, tucking his cleats in his bag. "I'm going into the woods to look at the bat box again. Anyone coming?"

"Yes," Jack and Brandon said in unison.

"Can't. My mom's here." Derek hopped up from sitting on the grass.

"No way," Wendy shook her head.

"Me either," Kim agreed.

Betsy tilted her head at Ava. "I'll go if you go …"

"Okay, let's go." Ava pulled her up.

They skirted the playground and entered the woods by the slide. The tall trees obscured the little daylight still left. Will used the flashlight on his phone and stared up at the bat box as the shadows crept closer. Jack shimmied a few feet up the tree and peeked in.

"There's something in here."

"Someone's coming!" Ava warned. Jack jumped down. They dove into the brush and froze upon hearing voices.

"Just climb up and see for yourself," they heard Boris say.

Will peeked between fronds of fern.

Behind Boris, Richie neared the tree with the bat box. "Seriously?"

"Just do it, Tan. You'll see."

"This better not be a joke." Richie climbed the tree, stuck his hand in the bat box and climbed down. Boris snatched one of the envelopes Richie was holding and pulled something out, waving the prize in the air.

"Open yours." Boris said.

Richie pulled out a piece of paper and squinted in the dim light. "That's it? That's all I have to do?"

"Yeah." Boris glanced around. "Let's go."

"But what's the point?"

"I don't know!"

"But who put the note in the bat box?"

"I DON'T KNOW! Look, Tan," Boris said as he clutched his hands into a fist. "I don't even know what your note says. My job was just to bring you here. Now, let's go!" Boris turned and stomped back out and Richie trailed behind him with his shoulders drooped, kicking leaves.

Will shook his head. "We have to keep an eye on Richie's desk now."

"Sounds risky. We don't know what his note says to do. Maybe something terrible." Brandon gestured toward Jack. "I vote we tell Richie we know he's getting paid to do something and put an end to this now."

"But if we tell him, we'll never find out who's paying people off. Don't you want to know?" Will stared at his friends. "Don't you want to know who's doing this?"

Jack, Ava, and Betsy said nothing. Brandon hesitated but nodded. "All right, fine."

"We won't take our eyes off Richie's desk," Will picked up his gear. "This time, we'll see who stashes the money."

Chapter 22

Will arrived at school early on Tuesday, eager to start the stakeout of Richie's desk. He saw Mr. Lockwood's purple bicycle in the usual spot. He poked his head into the classroom.

"Yes, Mr. Abbott?"

"Uh, good morning, Mr. Lockwood. Do you mind if I sit at my desk and study?"

"Study for what?"

"Well … you know … in case you give us a test … or something." Will shrugged. He waited for a response. Nothing. "Are you …?"

"Am I what?"

"Ever going to give us a test?"

"Eventually."

"Oh … well, okay. Then that's what I'll study for."

That wins the prize for the weirdest conversation with a teacher, Will thought. He unpacked his backpack and settled in for surveillance duty.

The minutes dragged on without any activity at Richie's desk. Will pretended to study his notes, watched the clock, and fiddled with his pen. Then he returned to ponder the contents of his science book when he caught Mr. Lockwood eyeing him.

Finally, the bell rang. As Mr. Lockwood walked up and down the rows placing a worksheet on everyone's desk, the class filed in. Will caught Jack's attention and nodded toward Richie's desk, signaling his turn to watch.

One by one the students took their seats. Then Richie rushed in, nearly tripping over his own feet to get to his seat to pounce on something. Jack glanced at Will as Richie bounced around his desk next to Boris.

Will's stomach clenched. "Impossible!" He mouthed to Jack, who threw his hands up in disgust.

Wendy came in and dropped her backpack. "You forgot to leave your phone home—" Upon seeing Will's expression, she followed his gaze across the room to where Richie and Boris were celebrating and slowly sank into her seat.

"Too late?" Her green eyes questioning.

Frustrated and disappointed, Will didn't answer.

Mr. Lockwood ordered Boris to his own desk. He strutted across the room, slowed to wiggle his new sneakers at Wendy, and passed Will with a smirk. Without thinking, Will stuck his foot out and tripped him. Wendy gasped and Boris yelped as he stumbled hard into Lucas's desk.

"Get off!" Lucas pushed Boris away and he fell backward, catching himself before he hit the floor. He popped back up and took a threatening step toward Will, only to trip again over his backpack. He landed in the aisle with his feet jutting in the air—to the class's amusement.

"Boris!" Mr. Lockwood's clipped tone cut through the snickers. "Is there a problem?"

"He tripped me!" Boris gestured angrily at Will from the floor.

Everyone looked at Will. He did not deny it. He just swung his legs back under his desk and put his head down. All eyes shifted to Mr. Lockwood as he slowly walked over to the first row. He said nothing. Boris picked himself up and dropped into his seat with an indignant grunt. Will's face burned. He could feel the weight of Mr. Lockwood's stare. He kept his head down waiting for the admonishment he knew was coming.

But there wasn't one. Mr. Lockwood's, "Take out your math books, please," redirected the class's attention—then Will tried to get control of his emotions. Tripping Boris was a stupid thing to do, he thought. It was something Boris himself would have done. Finally, he sighed and turned halfway back in his seat.

"Sorry," he whispered. No response. He didn't know if Boris heard him or not, but he felt a little better for the rest of the morning.

"That was classic!" Brandon said at lunchtime, joining Will, Jack, and Derek at their table. "Did you see Beefy's face?"

"I apologized," Will said. "I'm just tired of him flashing his sneakers in my face, and I was mad Richie got paid."

"I was sure Lockwood was gonna punish you," Jack said.

"Uh-uh. I saw his face," Derek frowned. "He actually seemed happy."

"He's weird anyway." Brandon looked around. "My mother is getting mad that he doesn't give tests or homework."

"Same," Will nodded. He spied Richie across the room. "I think Richie is actually telling everyone about the money. Look at them."

They followed his gaze to where Richie entertained a table of boys, which included Stuart and Micky. Everyone but Micky seemed impressed. But when Boris sauntered over, Richie stopped talking and Micky left.

"I just wish we knew how he got the money." Will banged the table.

"Easy," Brandon said, "someone stuck the envelope in his desk when you weren't looking."

"I'm telling you, no one came in." Will moved his chair over to make room as Wendy, Kimberly, Ava, and Betsy joined them.

"We have to stay inside for recess," Wendy said.

"What? Why?" Jack groaned.

"Miss Pierre said some loose dogs were running around town and the police don't want us going outside until they catch them."

"Loose dogs?" Jack scratched his head.

Wendy shrugged. "That's what she said."

"Hi guys! Can I sit here?" Richie had snuck up on their

table.

"Oh, su-u-ure," Jack said. He jumped up and grabbed an empty chair. "Join us!" He patted the seat. "So, what's new, Richie?" Jack clasped his hands on the table in front of him.

Richie smiled, a little uncertain at Jack's uncharacteristic welcome. He glanced around the table. "Well, I found a fifty-dollar bill in my desk this morning." He bounced in his seat, unable to contain his joy.

"Really?" Jack leaned in. "You don't say. That's amazing. Just like that? A fifty-dollar bill ... for no reason?"

"No, I had to do something," Richie said as he shrunk back. "But it was nothing really." Will saw Richie study everyone at the table and then realize eight pairs of accusing eyes stared back at him. Richie tried to flee, but Jack grabbed his arm.

"What'd you do, Richie? Smash a window? Let the air out of someone's tires?"

"Jack, don't," Betsy touched his arm.

"No," Richie put his hands up. "I would never! I just had to unlatch some back gates in the neighborhood."

"Oh really? That's all, Richie? Just unlatch some back gates? And what's gonna happen when some little kid gets lost because the parents don't know their back gate is unlatched?"

The color drained from Richie's face. "I-I didn't think ..."

"Why is Knobby here?" Kim pointed across the room where Officer Knobby spoke to Miss Pierre. He shook her hand, then paused to chat at a few tables.

"He's coming over here." Richie sunk in his seat as Knobby sauntered over.

"What's up, guys and girls?"

"Hey, Knobby," Will said.

"Too bad you had to stay inside on such a nice day, but better safe than sorry." He grinned.

"What happened?" Jack asked.

"Dogs running around town ... that's what happened. I think we found them all though." He scratched his bald head. "Weird. Owners swore their back gates were latched. But most people have security cameras in the front of their house, not the back, so they had no evidence to back up their claim." He observed Jack. "And speaking of cameras, check this out. Father Anthony sent this to me this morning." He pulled his cell phone out, tapped the screen a few times, and held it up. Through the dark and grainy video, the group watched the same hooded person cleaning the graffiti off the church wall.

Jack's mouth dropped open.

Knobby patted Jack's shoulder. "That's not easy stuff to remove. So, case closed. Have a great day, everyone. Maybe I'll see you at Sunday School." He winked and moved on.

Jack pushed his chair away from the table and stood. He scanned the cafeteria. He zeroed in on Micky and walked toward his table.

"I think Knobby likes Miss Chapman," Wendy said. The girls giggled.

"Who cares!" Richie ran his hands through his hair. "All those dogs got out because of me!" He stood, kicked his chair back, and stuck his hand in his front pocket to pull out his fifty-dollar bill. He threw the money on the table and stomped away without a backward glance.

Will snatched the fifty. "I'll put this with Micky's for now." He tucked the cash in his pocket and felt his phone vibrate.

"Whoa," Brandon said. "You took your phone?"

Will glanced at the screen and his eyebrow's shot up. "Oh, no!" He sank back into his seat. "My mom texted. Buster and Petunia are missing!"

Chapter 23

Will and Wendy met their mom and Mrs. Larson at school when the last bell rang. Mrs. Larson leaned from the passenger side window. "We haven't found them yet. We've been driving around for an hour."

"What happened?" Will asked even though he was sure he already knew what happened.

"Your mother and I were having tea. We put the dogs in your backyard to play. When we were finished, I went outside to get Petunia, but ..." Mrs. Larson sniffed. "... the back gate was open—and they were gone."

Mrs. Abbott patted her hand. "I'm sorry, Margery. I don't understand. I know that gate was closed."

Will turned to see their friends running over. "Guys, where's Derek? Did he leave yet? Maybe he can help us look."

Brandon coughed to get Will's attention. "He said Boris wanted to talk to him after school." Will's mouth dropped open. Brandon gave a nod and raised an eyebrow. "Yeah, so, he said he would catch up with us later."

Will closed his eyes as if to release the pressure building up in his brain. Boris wanted to talk to Derek? Was this the break he'd been praying for? He looked at Mrs. Larson's sad face. "Okay, give us the leashes. We'll find them."

Will threw one leash to Ava. "You guys look by the park. If you find them, put this on Buster. Petunia is small enough to carry."

Will sent a text to Derek, "Meet us at Memorial Field."

The route the boys took led them back through their neighborhood. As they approached the site of the Jamison fire, Will slowed. He walked over to the edge of the property and peered through the mass of vegetation.

"What? You don't think …"

Will hesitated. "Petunia has gone in there with Mrs. Larson."

"I don't know …" Brandon said.

Will found the entry point Mrs. Larson used. "I'll be right back." Pushing vines and tall grass aside, he plunged through and emerged into a clearing in front of the charred mansion. He whistled for the dogs.

"They're not here," he said to his friends. "You can come in … there's nothing here." Will walked through the dirt and patchy weeds kicking pieces of wood, stones, and broken glass. Something reflected from the rubble and he stooped to brush some dirt away revealing a section of red glass. He dug his fingers underneath until he dislodged a flat, round object geometrically-designed with colorful pieces of glass in a thin metal frame. He held it up to the sun.

"What's that?" Jack said from behind.

"A decoration." Will stuck the interesting piece in his jacket pocket.

"This isn't what I thought the place would look like," Brandon said, surveying the rubble.

"Yeah, me either," Jack said. "Let's go."

Stepping through the brush and back onto the sidewalk, they jogged to the field.

"I wonder what the Mayfield-Jamison feud was about," Will finally said.

"I think the problem started when the old Fern Valley rail line shut down," Brandon lowered his voice as they cut across the corner of Mrs. Larson's lawn. "Percy Mayfield wanted the job as stationmaster in Maple Grove, but Betsy's grandfather got the job instead. Some think Percy was jealous. That's what my dad told me, anyway—and he said there was never any proof of Mayfield starting the fire."

Jack hunched his shoulders. "Then why would they just disappear that night?"

"Sounds suspicious." Will agreed.

The boys found Derek walking the perimeter. "I don't see the dogs out here," he said.

Will sighed. "I was hoping ..."

Jack grabbed his arm. "Come on. We didn't even look in the woods yet." He led them to the same path they took on the day of the block party.

"Is it my imagination or are the ferns more beaten down than the last time we were here?" Brandon asked as they entered.

"You're right, Bran." Will parted some branches. "The path definitely seems more ... used." They stopped at the spot where they had found the stolen bikes.

Jack pointed. "Remember, Jon told us the train trestle was this way. The path is more worn down than before."

"Someone's been coming through here." Brandon said. No one moved. "Do you think the dogs would have come this far?"

Will activated the flashlight on his phone. "Let's find out." He raised his chin and called out, "Buster! Petunia!" They listened but heard nothing.

"Let's go in a little further." Derek waited for Jack's response.

"Yeah, and I still want to look at the train trestle." Jack marched ahead. "Let's go." They used their phones to light the way and hollered for the dogs as they trekked through the darkened path.

"Wait, I hear the stream," Brandon said. They continued until the dimly lit trail opened to a small clearing. The stream ran under the crumbling brick remains of the old train trestle in front of them. Will shined a light beam along the top of the structure. The letters FV were scrawled repeatedly all the way across.

"Fern Valley?" Derek guessed.

"Look what's underneath." Brandon pointed his flashlight.

YOU WILL PAY

Chapter 24

The boys stared at the trestle.

YOU WILL PAY

"Officer Travers was right. That is creepy."

Then they heard loud voices. "Buster! Petunia!"

"Sounds like Kim," Brandon said as Kimberly and her friends approached in the darkness.

"Brandon! Oh, thank goodness! We thought we were lost!"

"How did you get here?" Will shined his flashlight at their faces. "You were supposed to go to the park."

"We did," Ava said.

"And we just kept following this path, and here we are." Wendy squatted down to rest.

"Wow," Jack said. "All this time, we didn't know these woods were connected." He frowned at Betsy. "What happened to your arms?"

Betsy looked at the scratches on the inside of her arms and smiled. "Oh, I had to climb a tree. The one with the bat box."

"Yeah, you guys are not going to believe this!" Wendy's eyes grew round. "Betsy wanted to look in the bat box to see if there was anything inside, so she started to climb—"

"—and we heard someone coming so we jumped into the bushes," Kim said.

"But Betsy didn't have time to climb down, so she climbed up instead!" Ava leaned to the boys. "You'll never guess who showed up."

"Who?" Jack crossed his arms and furrowed his brow.

The girls cried in unison, "Mr. Lockwood!"

"What? Why?" Will's mouth hung open.

"Oh, Betsy found out!" The girls laughed.

"Tell us." Brandon stepped closer.

"Well ..." Kimberly wiped tears from her eyes. "... he climbed the tree a little and lifted the lid to the bat box—" She started laughing so hard she couldn't talk.

"—and a bat flew out!" Wendy said. The boys began laughing. "Wait—the story gets better."

"Mr. Lockwood fell backward and the bat flew up and scared poor Betsy ... and then, she fell ..." Ava waved her arms, "... right on top of Mr. Lockwood!"

"No way!" The boys stared at Betsy. "What did you say?"

"Well, first I said I was sorry. Then I asked him what he was doing, and he said he was looking at the bat box for a science lesson. Then he asked me why I was there—"

"—and Betsy told him she likes climbing trees." Wendy giggled sending everyone into hysterics.

"He didn't know you guys were in the bushes listening?" Derek squatted down.

"No, somehow we stayed quiet," Ava said, catching her breath. "And after he left, we started walking again and ended up here."

"We'll have to stick together." Will stopped and whispered. "Whoa, is that a dog?" The others followed his gaze and saw a shaggy white dog standing where the path branched off.

"Hello," Wendy murmured. Ava took a step forward. The dog stared at them and then, trotted back down the path.

"Another owner must be missing their dog too," Will said and they followed it.

The dog jumped off the trail and the group tried to keep up, stepping over large rocks and ducking under low hanging branches. At one point, the dog stopped so they could catch up.

"How nice of him to wait for us," Jack said, holding a branch up for the girls to scoot under.

"Yeah, I think he wants us to follow him." Wendy flicked her flashlight toward the dog.

"At least he's easy to see," Brandon said. "I've never seen a dog so white. He looks old."

The dog led them farther into the woods, waiting if they fell behind, but never letting them close enough to grab him. Finally, Will slowed. "We're not going to catch him, and I have no idea where we even are right now."

The dog stopped and turned back toward them.

"I think we should follow him a little farther," Betsy said. "He's definitely trying to tell us something." They resumed the chase. A short distance later, they heard barking.

"Sounds like Buster!" Will charged ahead. "Buster!" Buster sat with his tail thumping. Will ran over and hugged him, then stepped back, puzzled. "Why is he just sitting here like this?"

"Look," Brandon said. He shined his flashlight down a large hole behind Buster. By the light of the beam shining down into the deep opening, they saw Petunia's little face staring up at them.

"Oh no, poor Petunia!"

"I hope she's not hurt."

"Buster was guarding her."

"Good boy, Buster."

"How are we going to get her out?" Will said.

"I'll call Mom so she can tell Mrs. Larson we found them," Wendy said.

Will took out a bag of dog treats. He gave half to Buster and tossed the rest down to Petunia. "I see some other stuff down there. How did this hole get here anyway?"

"I bet it's an old well," Brandon said. "Didn't Mrs. Larson say the old train station was around here somewhere?"

"Mom said Dad and Knobby are on their way here," Wendy reported. "I sent them our location and Knobby is bringing a rope and basket. What time is it anyway?"

"Not even dinnertime. It just seems later because it's so dark in here," Ava said.

They sat in a circle around the hole to wait. Brandon turned to Derek. "Hey, what happened when you talked to Boris after school?"

Derek grinned. "He told me I couldn't tell anyone."

"No chance, buddy—spill everything!" Will said.

"I'm meeting him tomorrow night at the bat box. He said I could make a lot of money if I do a really important job. So, I asked what the 'really important job' was, and he said I'll find out tomorrow night."

Brandon sighed. "Maybe now we'll finally know what's going on around here."

Will's stomach grumbled when he saw a light beam approaching.

"Will?"

"Over here, Dad,"

Mr. Abbott and Officer Knobby came around the bend and into view.

"Wow—the old well," Knobby said as he walked toward them. "I'm sure we had this thing covered."

Mr. Abbott struggled to keep his balance as Buster jumped up on him, happily licking his face. "I can't believe you found them."

"That's right!" Wendy slapped her forehead. "We forgot about the white dog!"

"What white dog?" Knobby peered down into the hole at Petunia.

"We followed a white dog that led us here. We wouldn't have found our own without him."

"Hmmm, strange. I think we've found all the dogs reported missing." Knobby lowered the basket into the hole. "Come on, Petunia, jump in." Petunia clambered into the basket using her two front legs and pulled her body in behind her.

"I think she injured her back legs." Knobby passed her to Wendy. "She needs to go to the vet. But otherwise, not a bad ending. You kids are sure keeping me on my toes."

Brandon shined his light down the hole. "Knobby, something else is down there. I think it might be a metal box—maybe the cash box!"

Knobby peered down. "Looks like you're right. Listen, you kids take these dogs home. I'll call my guys over here and we'll check this out."

Chapter 25

Wednesday night, well before Derek's scheduled rendezvous, Will, Brandon, and Jack arrived at the park and settled themselves in a spot with a clear view of the bat box. They wore dark clothing for camouflage and, at Ava's suggestion, had their hoods pulled tightly around their faces so only their eyes showed.

"That will protect you from bugs too," she had said.

The girls had wanted to hide in the woods with them, but Will nixed the idea. "Boris would definitely see all of us." Instead, he gave them the job of watching from the playground and sending a text when they saw Boris approaching.

"Next time, we should set up a camera," Brandon said.

"Or we could ask Betsy to climb a tree and watch for us," Will said, and laughed.

"She would too," Jack said with admiration. "She's not scared of anything."

Will nodded. "Wendy said the same thing."

"She told me why she and her uncle moved back to Fern Valley." Jack began to whisper, "He's a private investigator, and he's been tracking the Mayfields. One of their fingerprints was found on the stolen bikes."

Will's phone lit up. "Beefy's coming." They crouched down and watched a bouncing beam of light grow closer. Boris's rotund figure appeared. He charged forward and picked up a stick to reach high and tap the bat box. Satisfied to find no bats inside, he dropped the stick and went back out to the playground. A few minutes passed. Boris reappeared, followed by Derek.

"Okay, Harrison, go up there."

"What's up there?"

"Your job. Just climb up and stick your hand in the box."

Boris shined his light on the tree. Derek found a knot to use as a foothold. He boosted himself and grabbed a branch. He slid his free hand into the opening and felt around.

"There's nothing in here."

Will's heart sank. Nothing in there? Then he heard Jack snicker.

"What do you mean—?" Boris grabbed the bottom of Derek's sweatshirt and pulled him down. With some difficulty, he hefted himself high enough and struggled to fit his pudgy hand in the box. When he jumped down, he was holding two envelopes. He glared at Derek.

"Sorry," Derek said.

Boris shoved one envelope in his pocket and one at Derek. "Open it."

Derek opened his envelope and studied the piece of paper in his hand. He stared at Boris. "I have to do what this says and then I get paid?"

"Yes." Boris turned to leave.

"Wait."

"What."

"Give me your sneakers."

"What?"

"Give me your sneakers. Those are my instructions." Derek read his note and enunciated each word. "Take Boris's sneakers and drop them in a donation bin."

Will gaped. Brandon clamped his hand over his mouth. They could both feel Jack's body convulsing in silent laughter.

Boris snatched the paper out of Derek's hand and scowled at the instructions.

"Sorry, but you said—"

"I know what I said." Boris dropped to untie his sneakers. Without looking at Derek again, he pulled them off, threw them down, and stomped out of the woods in his socks.

Will and his friends waited until Wendy texted before busting out of the bushes in hysterics. "That was brilliant!" Will said to Derek.

Derek pointed at Jack. "His idea. I actually had to practice with a straight face."

Will gave Jack a fist bump. "Thanks, guys." Wendy and her friends joined them.

"Boy, did Boris look mad," Betsy said.

Derek told them about the switched note. When the laughter died down, he held up the real one.

Wendy read the message aloud. "Get the Clean Water Fund jar from the church and put it on Mr. Lockwood's desk tomorrow morning." She slapped her hands on her hips. "We can't! The Clean Water Fund donation is for the African village."

"Not to mention, the jar has a ton of money. We could face a felony," Brandon said.

"And why Mr. Lockwood's desk? Is someone trying to frame him?" Kim said.

Will's mind raced. "This says tomorrow morning, which doesn't give us much time, but I have a plan. I think we can find out who's behind this game."

Chapter 26

Thursday morning, when the bell rang, the eighth-grade students entered the classroom with their usual chatter. For the second day in a row, Richie went straight to Will's desk. He did not seem to care that Boris could hear everything he said.

"How's Buster?"

"Still fine, Richie."

"How's Petunia?"

"She's in a back brace, … but she'll be fine, Richie."

"I'm really sorry."

"I know you are. I'll let you know if anything changes, Richie."

Will and his friends only had the morning to sneak the Clean Water Fund jar onto Mr. Lockwood's desk, and the clock was ticking.

Richie nodded, glared at Boris, and went to his desk. Boris sat slumped and had no comment. Will resisted the urge to ask him where his sneakers were.

While the class worked on problems, Mr. Lockwood walked up and down the aisles, checking their progress. Will raised his hand to create a diversion.

"Mr. Lockwood?"

"Yes, Mr. Abbott?"

"Could you come over here? I don't understand this problem."

Mr. Lockwood walked over to the first row and looked at Will's work, his back to the rest of the class.

"Uh, can you show me how to put this fraction in lowest terms?"

Mr. Lockwood frowned at him. "You do this problem the same way you did the other ones."

"Oh." Will saw movement in the middle row. "Well, can you please show me?"

Annoyed, he grabbed Will's pencil and scribbled numbers on the paper. While the class worked, Derek wasted no time in placing the jar on Mr. Lockwood's desk and scooting back to his seat.

"Thank you, Mr. Lockwood."

Now they just had to wait. Will had no idea what to expect next. Would someone stand up and yell accusations? Would the real culprit come in and try to steal the jar off his desk? Something had to happen soon. Mr. Lockwood would undoubtedly see the brightly painted and clearly labeled Clean Water Fund jar and wonder how it got there. If he asked, the plan was for Wendy to take responsibility and invite him to donate.

When lunchtime came, Will was reluctant to leave the room. Someone had to keep an eye on the jar.

"Um, excuse me, Mr. Lockwood?"

"What now, Mr. Abbott?"

"Do you mind if I stay in here during lunch and study?"

"Study for what?"

"Well, you know, in case you ever—"

"—give a test? No, you may not. There are no tests planned at this time, so you will go to the cafeteria." And he locked the classroom door behind them.

"Nice try," Brandon chuckled when they sat to eat. "'No, you may not.'" He mimicked Mr. Lockwood making Kim and Wendy giggle.

"I thought the jar would be gone already," Ava said, unwrapping her sandwich.

Jack nodded. "Me too. I just wish I could see the person's face when they open it. That one looks exactly like the real one, Wendy."

"Thanks. I still had all the materials at home from when Father Anthony asked me to make the real one."

"I never even got paid," Derek said. "I bet he's broke."

"Right. I bet he used all the money in the cash box," Brandon said, "and then tossed it down the hole. That's why you got that task, Derek—because he needs more money."

"You guys are assuming the thief is a he. Maybe the he is a she," Wendy said.

"Well, someone is in for a major surprise." Will noticed Boris sulking from across the cafeteria. "Beefy is mad about something. I don't think he's angry about the sneakers. I wonder if his envelope was empty last night."

They went outside for recess and Jack harassed everyone until they agreed to play basketball. Kimberly convinced Boris to keep score and Will noticed, for the first time in weeks, the whole class played together with no hard feelings as Mr. Lockwood watched from his monitor post.

After recess, reality settled in when Mr. Lockwood unlocked the classroom door. Will immediately scanned the desktop. Derek nodded at Will. The colorful jar was gone. Had someone found the wad of play money inside? Had someone read the note Derek tucked into the jar?

LET'S END THIS. MEET ME AT THE BAT BOX FRIDAY NIGHT AT 7.

And—would someone show up?

Chapter 27

Boris fumed all day Friday. He unfolded the message he had found in the usual spot in his desk that morning and reread it.

IF YOU WANT YOUR MONEY BRING BETSY JAMISON TO THE BAT BOX STRAIGHT FROM SCHOOL TODAY.

Boris sat perplexed. What was he supposed to do, walk over to her and say, "Hey, Betsy, do you want to go to the bat box with me after school today?" And why should he bother anyway? Last time he brought Derek, he got nothing but an empty envelope and he had to give up his sneakers—even though he never cared about the sneakers. He just liked using them to make Abbott mad.

Boris stared at the back of Will's head and thought about how the job had all started with him on the first day of school. He stopped at the park on the way home and heard someone call his name from the woods. When he went in to investigate, he saw an envelope sticking out of the bat box with his name on it and with fifty bucks in it and a note saying, "Want more? Bring Will Abbott's new sneakers here Friday night." Easier said than done. What was he supposed to do? Steal them off his feet? But he had liked the idea of another fifty-dollar bill. So, he managed to get inside the Abbott's house with his mother and grab them. Then after each task, the fifties just kept coming and he got to sit back and watch the kids in the class turn on each other. Priceless! But, he brooded, the strife he created among his classmates never lasted long. They forgave each other. Blah-blah-blah.

Now, the taskmaster wanted him to bring Betsy. Boris had no idea who was paying him, and that made him a little nervous. He had never been asked to bring a girl before. Something didn't seem right about that request—even in broad daylight.

Boris looked across the room to where Betsy sat. He had considered talking to her at lunch, but she was in deep conversation with Jack the whole time. Now it was almost time to go home. He redirected his gaze to the front of the room and caught Mr. Lockwood staring at him. Boris ducked away. Weirdest. Teacher. Ever. They never did much in class, but today they literally did nothing. Didn't touch a book all day.

The bell rang. Boris scanned the note again and smashed it into a hard ball. He wanted the money. He'd do another deed—but he'd better get paid this time. He waited until most of the students had left, and then followed Betsy.

"Uh, Betsy?"

"Oh, hi, Boris."

"Have you ever seen the bat box?"

Betsy stared at him. "Um … do you mean the bat box by the park?"

"Yeah, yeah. I'm heading over to check out the bats." Boris waited to see if she would invite herself. She didn't.

"Well, wouldn't they be sleeping now? Maybe you shouldn't disturb them."

Boris clenched his teeth and tried not to sound desperate. "Yeah, yeah, I know. But sometimes, I just stand there … and look at it."

Betsy blinked. "Oh, I see."

He held his breath. She glanced around and saw her friends had left and hesitated. Finally, she said, "Okay, I'll go and look at the bat box with you."

Boris was glad the walk to the park was only five minutes. He had no idea what to talk to her about. Luckily, he didn't have to worry. She did all the talking. Unfortunately, she chattered about Sunday School stuff, his least favorite subject.

"So, what commandment do you have for the Sunday School project?" Betsy skipped along.

"Five."

"Oh, 'thou shall not kill.'"

"Yeah, I'm not planning to."

"You know, Boris," Betsy said, "that's not the only way you can break that commandment. It means loving your neighbor as you would have them love you."

Boris grunted.

"Like for instance, do you bully?"

Was she kidding? He could see the park ahead. Almost there. Boris wondered what would happen and he started to get nervous. He had better get paid this time. One thing was certain, he thought, as she prattled on about the fifth commandment—Betsy was way too righteous to do anything wrong for money. The taskmaster was in for a big disappointment.

"So, really, Boris, any time you seek to hurt people, you're breaking the commandment. Oh, we're here already."

They entered the woods and followed the path. Boris craned his neck and peered through the trees to get a glimpse of the bat box.

"And one more thing, Boris," Betsy said.

"What?"

"It's never too late to change."

Change? Why would he change?

"Oh, I see the bat box," Betsy whispered. "Let's not disturb it."

Boris scowled. He didn't see any envelopes sticking out. Maybe they were inside. "I have to check something."

"No, Boris, don't!"

Ignoring her, he found a foothold. Just as he started to pull himself up, a bat poked its head out of the box. Boris reared back, lost his footing, and landed on the ground.

Instantly, Mr. Lockwood crashed out of the brush. He scooped Betsy up before Boris could react, threw her over his shoulder, and charged back down the path in the direction he came from.

Splayed on the ground in shock, Boris heard her screaming as they disappeared.

Chapter 28

"Do you think Mr. Lockwood was weirder than usual today?" Brandon asked on the way to the park Friday night. "He just sat at his desk the whole day."

"He creeps me out," Kim pulled the hood of her sweatshirt up, prompting Wendy and Ava to do the same. Even though it was still September, a chill hovered in the air.

"My mother is getting really mad," Wendy said. "He doesn't answer her emails."

"What does she email him about?" Derek asked.

"No tests or homework," Will answered. "What happens if we don't learn anything the whole year? Didn't Jon say high school is really hard, Jack?"

Jack didn't answer. He trudged behind. Ava glanced at Will and shook her head.

He's probably upset Betsy couldn't come with us tonight, Will thought. He saw the park ahead. "Okay, let's slow down and go over the plan."

"Do we even have a plan?" Brandon asked.

"Yes." Will elbowed him. "Derek waits at the bat box. We stake out the area and send a text if we see anyone coming. Then we follow him in and confront him."

"Yeah!" Wendy put up her fists in imaginary confrontation. "Who do you think you are, stealing mission money?"

"Easy, girl," Derek laughed.

"But this could be dangerous. We have no idea who is doing this," Ava said. "There is a lot of money in the real Clean Water Fund jar. Whoever wants it might be desperate."

Jack reached into his pocket and pulled out a pocketknife.

"Jack," Kimberly gasped. "We can't stab someone."

"Relax. No one's gonna get hurt. I'm prepared for an emergency ... in case we get tied up."

The wind picked up and Brandon pulled his hood on. "Like Ava said, we have no idea who we're dealing with. Let's go."

Wendy froze. "I'm nervous."

"Come on." Will pulled her. "We have our cell phones. We can call 911 if we have to."

Derek went into the woods alone. Will saw Jack slip him the knife. The rest of the group huddled together by the jungle gym. Wendy and Ava hopped in place to keep warm.

Will pulled his hat down over his ears. "Did you bring a hat?" he said to Jack.

Jack plucked at his jacket. "This is pretty warm." He noticed Brandon shifting from one foot to the other. "What's wrong with you?"

"Nothing," Brandon said.

"His sneakers are too small," Kimberly informed them.

"Come on, man, it's time," Will laughed. His phone buzzed. He looked at the text on the screen and frowned. "My mom says Mrs. Bobrick called looking for Boris. She hasn't seen or heard from him since he left for school this morning. That's weird, even for Beefy." Will texted back that they hadn't seen him. Another buzz. This time the sender was Derek.

Derek: You guys had better come in here.

They raced in. Derek held up a cell phone. "Look what I found. I saw something light up under the leaves." He pressed a button and the home screen lit up with missed calls and text messages. "This is Boris's. His mother's been texting him all afternoon. Even she calls him Beefy."

"Sure—how did you think he got his nickname?" Will said. "She always refers to him as 'my little Beefy.'"

Brandon raised his eyebrows and shrugged. "I thought you made the name up."

Will grimaced. "I would never call someone—"

Jack held his hand up. "Listen. I hear something."

They stood still.

Will shook his head.

"Listen," Jack said. "Someone's calling."

Will took his hat off and strained to hear. Above the whoosh of the autumn wind and the rustle of fallen leaves, they heard a faint, "Help!"

"Where is the voice coming from?" Derek scrutinized the area.

They heard the call again. Jack shined his flashlight beam around until he found the path which led deeper into the woods. He charged in.

"Jack, wait for us," Wendy called.

They sprinted through rough terrain trying to keep up with Jack until they lost sight of him.

"Help me!" The voice sounded louder than before.

"There," Will pointed. They ran toward the yelling.

"This is the same path we took when we were looking for the dogs," Ava panted. "We're heading toward the train trestle."

They reached the stream. "Which way? I don't hear anything," Brandon said.

Will pointed. "The trestle is that way."

"Over here," Jack called.

Jack stood next to the hole they had found Petunia in. Jack shined his light in the hole and they peered down. Boris stared up at them.

"Boris!" Kimberly crouched down. "Are you hurt?"

"No, but I'm stuck."

"How did he even get down there?" Wendy said.

"We'll never get him out." Will pulled out his phone.

"We need a ladder," Derek said.

"He must be freezing." Kimberly clasped her hands together and shivered.

Derek took his jacket off and dropped it down. Boris struggled to wrap it around his broad shoulders.

Will poked his head over the side. "Boris, we will never be able to get you out. I'm calling for help."

"Oh, yeah," Derek said, "and here." He tossed Boris's phone down to him. "Call your mom."

"Don't leave me here!" Boris whimpered. "He's still out there."

Will tensed his brow. "What? Who's still out there, Boris?"

"Mr. Lockwood—and he has Betsy!"

"Betsy? What? Mr. Lockwood has Betsy?"

"Yes! He kidnapped her …" He started to cry.

Ava gripped Will's arm. "He's delirious. Call someone, quick."

"… and I tried to follow them, but then I fell in this hole!" He blubbered.

Jack leaned over the hole. "Boris, calm down. No one stole Betsy. She went back to Los Angeles."

"No," Wendy gasped.

Jack nodded. "She's gone," he whispered. "She left after school today."

"But she didn't say goodbye." Kim's lip quivered.

"I found this note in my pocket when I got home from school." Jack held a small piece of paper under Will's light.

To my Fern Valley friends,

I am going back to Los Angeles today. I want you to know how much fun I had here. Thank you for being so nice to me and making me feel welcome.

Your friend, Betsy

"What? How could she just—hey," Brandon pointed, "there's the white dog again."

They spun around and saw the same white dog that had led them to Buster and Petunia, standing on the path staring at them.

"Hello," Will said. He put his hand out in a friendly gesture. The dog turned away and trotted down the path. Then returned, stared at them, and barked.

"I think he wants us to follow him," Brandon said.

The four boys approached the dog. His tail wagged and he began to lead them. Will called to the girls who stayed behind as the boys followed the dog. "Stay with Boris until help gets here!"

Chapter 29

The dog turned off the trail leading the chase through dense, overgrown forest. "Oh, come on. Does he think this is a game?" Brandon huffed.

"How do your feet feel?" Will grinned.

"Shut up."

The underbrush started to thin. They could see the dog had stopped ahead. They stepped out of the woods and into a clearing with a small building.

"What is this place?" Jack banged his flashlight on his knee. "The battery is dead."

Will used the flashlight on his phone. Over the doorway of the ramshackle structure was a sign. He took a step closer, trying to make out the faded lettering. "Fern Valley Rail," he read. "This is the old train station."

The dog pushed the door open with his snout and slipped inside. The door creaked closed.

"Should we go in?" Brandon asked.

"Yes," Jack said. "Where's my knife?" Derek tossed it to him.

Once inside, by the light of his cell phone, Will noticed a purple bicycle laying on the floor. He nudged Brandon and pointed. "That's Mr. Lockwood's bike."

"Guys," Jack said. "Look around." He put his hand on the wall and flicked a switch. The room lit up the makeshift living quarters.

Derek stared at the floor. Play money was scattered everywhere. He crouched down. "Look at this." He held up a piece of broken glass. Will's heart hammered in his chest as he recognized the shattered remains of the fake Clean Water Fund jar Wendy had prepared for their scheme.

Brandon, sidestepping a sleeping bag and pillow, ambled over to a desk. "Whoa—this is our schoolwork. He must be living here. Let's go."

Jack flicked the light switch again leaving them standing in a room illuminated by moonlight. The white dog whimpered by a closet door, tail thumping.

"Wait." Jack put his finger to his lips and pointed at the closet. Broken glass crunched under his feet as he tiptoed across the floor. He put his hand on the knob and signaled to Will to turn on his light. He held up his hand to count and the boys braced themselves—one, two, three. He flung the door open. Inside was Betsy.

The boys gaped at her as her tearful eyes lit up and she seemed to smile through a bandana tied around her mouth. They untied the bandana and used the pocketknife to carefully cut the tape binding her wrists and ankles.

"It was Mr. Lockwood," she said as soon as she could speak.

"We know. Are you okay?" Jack pulled her up. "Did he hurt you?"

"No," Betsy said. "Thank you for saving me."

When they hustled outside, Will used the last of his phone battery to text Wendy.

WILL: Did the police get there yet?

WENDY: Yes.

WILL: Is Boris out?

WENDY: Yes.

WILL: Send them here.

He sent their location, and they sat on a log to wait. Betsy shivered and Jack unzipped his sweatshirt and put it around her shoulders as the dog climbed onto her lap. Will shivered too, but he wasn't sure if the reason was the cold or finding out Betsy had been kidnapped by his teacher.

Betsy recounted the kidnapping. "… and he told me he knew my family." Betsy whispered, "And he said this is my dog."

Jack frowned. "You mean he gave the dog to you?"

"I don't know …"

Will reached over to pat the dog. "Well, he's the reason we found you."

"He said this town was mean to his family and he came back to cause trouble."

Jack cracked a stick over his knee. "He definitely did that."

"Then he said he realized he was wrong … and he was sorry … and he wanted me to deliver a message."

"What message?"

"He said his father is innocent." She shuddered.

"I guess his name isn't Mr. Lockwood," Brandon said. "Should we call him Mr. Mayfield?"

Jack took the note out of his pocket and passed it to Betsy. "We thought you left Fern Valley."

Betsy read the note. "Mr. Lockwood wrote this."

"Mr. Lockwood …" Brandon shook his head. "… who knew?"

They saw beams of light flitting about through the trees.

"Over here," Will called. He squinted in the glare as a light flooded the area.

"Now what fun have you kids cooked up?" Officer Knobby approached and eyed Betsy. "Your uncle is looking for you."

All the teens explained the kidnapping and the robbery evidence. Knobby took two of the officers inside the train station to investigate.

Will saw Knobby flick his radio and command dispatch to connect him to Principal Thomas immediately and to notify Jerry Jamison that they found his niece.

"Will do," they heard the dispatcher say. "And we also just got an anonymous tip about someone in trouble at the old train station. The caller said to check the closet."

They all stared at Betsy.

"I guess I couldn't deliver his message if I was never found," she shrugged.

Betsy waited with Knobby for her uncle to come while an officer led the boys back to the park where the girls were waiting.

Wendy observed Will's face. "What happened?"

"You guys are not gonna believe this …"

Chapter 30

On Saturday morning, Will met Betsy on the sidewalk near the site of the Jamison house fire.

"Thanks for meeting me here, Will."

"Are you sure you want to go in there?"

"Yes, but not alone, and I know you've already been in."

Will ran his hand along the bushy overgrowth at the edge of the property as they walked. "What did your uncle say about Mr. Lockwood?"

"He asked if Mr. Lockwood has one blue eye and one brown eye. It's a Mayfield trait. Then he said Mr. Lockwood must be one of Percy Mayfield's sons, which we figured—and he showed me this." She pulled out a yellowed photograph.

Will studied the image of the beaming red-haired baby sitting in a chair with a white puppy. His brows shot up. "Is that—?"

"Yes, we think the puppy is the white dog. This proves the Mayfields were involved somehow. Uncle Jerry took this picture while he was visiting, a few weeks before the fire. We were in the guest room." She pointed to the window behind the chair in the photo. "The investigator's report shows the fire started in the guest room under that window."

"How?" Will studied the picture. "Unless someone threw something through the window that knocked over a candle or … wait—look at this!" His pointed to a decoration hanging on the window in the photo. "I found that thing … last time I was here … sticking out of the dirt." He fished around in his jacket pocket and pulled the object out. "Here."

Betsy held the colorful piece of glass in the palm of her hand. "It's a suncatcher." She pressed the piece to her cheek as they walked.

"There's nothing in there, you know." He stopped when he found the gap in the mass of grass and vines. He pushed his way through with Betsy close behind, but before they reached the clearing, they heard voices and ducked as they peered in.

"Mr. Lockwood," Betsy whispered.

Will gawked. "… with Mrs. Larson." He strained to hear.

"I just wish I could find something that would prove my father was innocent." Mr. Lockwood kicked rubble around as he spoke. "I searched the mansion too. Nothing."

"I don't know why you can't just go to the police and tell them what happened that day, Otis."

Otis? Will thought.

"It's too late, Aunt Margery."

Aunt Margery?

"I've caused too much trouble in Fern Valley, and I'll be arrested. I was angry when my father died. He was blamed for that fire and was never able to prove his innocence. I came back because I wanted revenge."

Will glanced at Betsy. Her eyes were round while she leaned to listen.

"I'm sorry about your father, Otis." Mrs. Larson waved her hands around wildly as she spoke. Petunia sat at her feet and whined. "But it was no secret that my cousin was bitter about losing the stationmaster job to Walter Jamison. What else would people think when they died in a suspicious fire—especially when Percy was seen on the property and ran?"

"He was trying to help them. We had gone there because he wanted to say he was sorry. When we got there, the place was on fire."

Mrs. Larson raised a hand to her mouth. "Then he ran to my house …"

Will felt Betsy lean closer. She began to lose her balance, but before could catch her, she fell through the bushes. She tried to scramble back.

"Wait." Otis stepped toward Betsy, shoulders sagging in defeat as Will climbed through next to her. His voice cracked. "I tried to save them. I really did."

Will saw Mrs. Larson back away and disappear out to the street.

"I kept yelling and finally I saw Walter at an upstairs window. He said they were trapped."

Betsy let out a sob.

"Then I heard him yell, 'Son, catch her!' He leaned out the window with a baby, pleading, 'Please, son, catch her!'" Otis nodded at Betsy's shocked face. "He dropped you right into my arms ... and disappeared. I could hear the sirens and because of the history between our families, I thought I would be accused so I put you down in a safe spot. Then I ran off. I never realized your puppy followed me."

Officers Knobby and Travers pushed through the clearing with Mrs. Larson, and Otis stepped toward them with his arms straight out in front of him.

"Otis Mayfield, you are under arrest for kidnapping, burglary, vandalism ..." Officer Travers recited as he snapped on the handcuffs.

Otis gazed at Will and Betsy. "I'm sorry. I should have learned from my father's mistake and not held a grudge all these years."

Will stuck his hands in his pockets and gaped while watching the officers lead Mr. Lockwood away. He sat on the ground with Betsy. "Are you okay?"

A single tear ran down her cheek. "Wow, my grandfather's last act was to save me."

Will nodded, Walter Jamison's final words ringing in his head ... Son catch her! ... Suncatcher.

"The Suncatcher! Wait!" Everyone turned to Will. He jumped up. "Betsy, where's that picture?"

She pulled the photo out of her pocket along with the decoration Will had found.

"Look at this." He touched a finger to the window ornament in the picture. "The suncatcher ... I learned in science if the sun's rays are magnified enough, they could start a fire." He pointed to the one Betsy was holding.

"If the fire really started here, this could have acted like a magnifying glass."

"Hmmm ... I'll have to show this to our fire investigator." Officer Travers collected the photo and the suncatcher as Knobby patted Will's shoulder. "You may have something here, Will."

"That might prove my father was innocent." Otis studied the officers.

"Otis, we never had any evidence your father started the fire. We only wanted to question him as a witness. The rumor started because he disappeared." Knobby shook his head as he cleared the way to the street. "But, yes, I guess the rumor could be dispelled if an official cause of fire is released."

Otis flashed a hopeful expression at Will before entering the cop car.

Chapter 31

After mass on Sunday, Wendy stood with Father Anthony outside the church holding the original Clean Water Fund jar. Even though it was clearly overflowing, they wanted to give the parishioners one last chance to donate on the last day of the drive. Will stood by with Brandon and Jack and watched Wendy talk about the mission to bring clean water to poor villages in Africa to anyone who would listen.

"Uh, excuse me, Miss," Will said. Wendy refrained from giggling. "We'd like to make a contribution."

Father Anthony amused expression turned to surprise when Jack and Brandon each pushed a fifty-dollar bill—the ones rejected by Micky and Richie—into the jar.

"Thank you, sirs," she bowed, knowing Mr. Lang had refused to take the bills back.

Then Will dropped his twenty-dollar bill into the jar. "Will, that's your money! You found it fair and square."

"I never felt like the money belonged to me," he said to Wendy. "I'd rather make a donation."

"Then, thank you." She smiled.

Will leaned toward Father Anthony. "I have some things I need to talk about ... some things I did ... not now ..."

Father Anthony nodded. "Anytime, Will."

Miss Chapman tried to contain the huge smile on her face. "Do we have any prayer requests today?" she asked as her Sunday School students bowed their heads.

Betsy's hand shot up. "I want to pray for Mr. Lockwood."

"That's very nice."

Ava raised her hand. "My abuela in Mexico is sick."

"And my grandma is having surgery this week," Kenny added.

"Thank you for finding my dog this week when he got lost," Wendy said.

"That I get a brother this time," Brandon said. The class laughed.

Will peered around the room and saw that Boris was not in class. "I have a special intention for someone I know who could use some prayers."

"Okay," Miss Chapman said. "Let's—"

"I have an intention." Knobby stood in the doorway gazing at Miss Chapman. "I would like to thank God this nice lady has agreed to be my wife."

The class gasped, and Miss Chapman blushed. She bowed her head, smiled, and then prayed. When she was done the class jumped up to congratulate them and admire her engagement ring.

"Okay, back to work, now," she laughed. "I'm giving you one more day to work on your Commandment project. Presentations start next week."

Will and Ava moved their desks together. "I got a new turtle yesterday," Ava said.

"What happened to the old one?"

"I gave him to my little brother. He really liked him. I named the new one Freckles."

Will patted his own freckled cheeks and laughed as Knobby approached.

"The fire investigator is very interested in your theory, Will. Don't be surprised if he calls you to help with some experiments when he reconstructs the scene."

Will just bobbed his head, eyes wide.

"One thing is certain, though," Knobby said. "You won't see Otis Mayfield at Fern Valley Middle School again. But," he winked, glancing over at Miss Chapman, "you might see someone else."

On Monday morning, the eighth graders and their parents attended an announcement in the school gym. They learned of the kidnapping and robbery and how the police held Otis Mayfield in the Fern Valley jail while he awaited sentencing.

Principal Thomas stepped forward and spoke to the parents. "All I can say is … I should have taken your concerns more seriously. I'll hire a suitable replacement."

"Great," Boris grumbled, "now we'll have to do real work."

Will snuck a peek at Boris. He looked like his usual boorish self, fully recovered from his ordeal in the woods.

On the way to the classroom, Will admired Brandon's new sneakers. "What did you do with the old ones?"

"I'm saving them in case I get a little brother." Brandon grinned.

Will just shook his head and Derek handed him a bag. "Speaking of sneakers, return Boris's for me. They were never mine to take."

Will dropped the bag on Boris's desk and sat. As the classroom filled, Boris lagged, but Will heard the surprised grunt from behind when Boris opened the bag. Will glanced back.

"What was that, Abbott?" He leaned forward and growled as Will suppressed a smile. "Some big joke? Real funny."

After school, Will walked home with Ava. "We have our first soccer game tonight. Can you come?"

"Definitely … go Tigers!"

"Okay, great … Say 'hi' to Freckles for me." The words tumbled out before he could shut his mouth. Stupid, stupid, stupid, he thought. He grinned while he walked away.

As he neared his house, Will noticed how the leaves were already changing colors. September was almost over. What secrets would October hold? Will knew one thing for certain—God would help him every step of the way.

About the Author

Doreen McAvoy is a librarian and Theology teacher, a job which combines two of her favorite things—books and God. With the publication of this, her debut novel, Secrets in September, Doreen can add author to the list. Her favorite job, though, is that of wife and mother.

Doreen lives in New York with her husband, Greg, and four sons, Patrick, Greg, Chris, and Ryan. A reluctantly retired soccer mom, Doreen now spends her spare time reading and writing, and given the chance to travel, Doreen will choose Maine every time! Doreen regularly posts middle grade book recommendations on her website at https://doreenmcavoy.com where you can also sign up for her newsletter.